Wall Of Conquest

The Princess Maura Tales
Saga of the de Magela Family

Book Four

Abigail Keam

Worker Bee Press

Worker Bee Press
P.O. Box 485
Nicholasville, KY 40340

Acknowledgements

Thanks to my editors,
Patti DeYoung and Jacy Mackin

Artwork by Karin Claesson
www.karinclaessonart.com

Book jacket by Peter Keam
Author's photograph by Peter Keam

Also by Abigail Keam

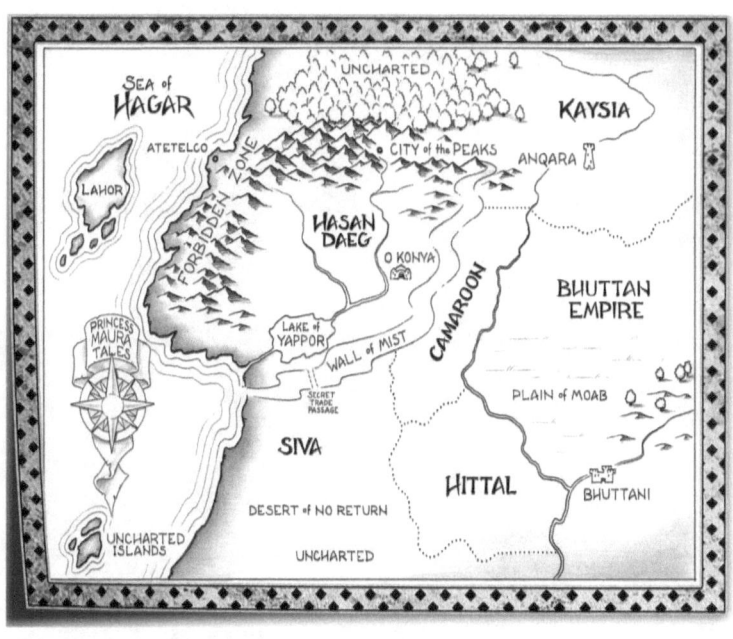

The Princess Maura Series Glossary

Abisola de Magela (character) – ninth queen of Hasan Daeg and mother of Princess Maura

Aga (character) – term for king of the Bhuttanians

Akela (character) – homeless Bhuttanian waif who serves KiKu and Timon

Alexanee (character) – top Bhuttanian general, illegitimate older brother of Dorak

Anqara (place) – ancient cultural and banking city located in country of Kaysia

Atetelco (place) – former capital of the Dinii located in the Forbidden Zone

Beca (character) – Princess Maura's pony

Benzar (character) – gray male hawk from secret society that protects Maura

Bes Amon Ptah (character) – Moab prince hiding under the name of Timon Ben Ibin Moab

Bhutta (character) – female deity of Bhuttanians, wife of Bhuttu

Bhuttan (place) – country ruled by Zoar and his son, Dorak

Bhuttani (place) – capital of Bhuttan

Bhuttanians (characters) – nomadic people who rose to world domination under the leadership of Zoar

Bhuttu (character) – male deity of Bhuttanians whose worship calls for the sacrifice of one's life

Bilboa (characters) – race of people with red eyes who see in the dark

Bird People (characters) – the Dinii who were Overlords of Kaseri

Black Cacodemon (character) – evil wizard of Bhuttu

Blue and gold – royal colors of the Hasan Daegians

Blue Queen (character) – nickname for Maura

Boaeps – small domesticated hopping animals

Borax (both plural and singular) – bison-like animals with sharp blades down their spines

Camaroon (place) – borders Hasan Daeg, absorbed by Bhuttanian Empire

Cappet (character) – petty thief, controls eastern part of Bhuttani

Caromate plant – provides hypnotic mist when leaves are pressed

Chaun Maaun (character) – prince of the Dinii and son of the Dinii Empress Gitar

City of the Peaks (place) – city on top of highest peak in Hasan Daeg where the Dinii live

Colla – nuts from the colla tree, brewed for teas

de Magela (characters) – name of ruling family in Hasan Daeg

Dini (character) – singular of Dinii

Dinii (characters) – ancient rulers of Kaseri, formerly called Overlords, human-like beings covered with feathers who fly

Divigi (character) – spiritual leader of the Dinii and uncle to Empress Gitar

Dorak (character) – son of Zoar, aga of the Bhuttanians

Duchy of Enos (place) – estate passed down through the family of Iasos, husband of Queen Abisola

Duke Enos (character) – father of Iasos

Dyanna (character) – princess born to Maura and Dorak

Everlynd (character) – duchess of Enos and sister of Prince Consort Iasos

Forbidden Zone (place) – former home of the Dinii, cursed by both the Dinii and Hasan Daegians

Gitar (character) – empress of the Dinii and Hasan Daegians

Gootee – duck-like animal

Great Death – name given to the practice of Hasan Daegian queens willing themselves to die

Great Mother – title of respect for older women or those in power, including queens of Hasan Daeg

Hasan Daeg (place) – peaceful agricultural country ruled by the Dinii and the de Magela family

Hasan Daegian betrothal (custom) – woman asks man permission to court by kissing man's hand; if man wishes to engage, he returns the kiss; woman gives man flowers

Hasan Daegians (characters) – peaceful agricultural people who were former slaves of the Dinii

Hetmaan (character) – Bhuttanian term for Spymaster KiKu

Hittal (place) – country conquered by Zoar, land of KiKu the Hetmaan

House of Magi (place) – ancient residence of scholars in Anqara

Iasos (character) – consort of Queen Abisola and father of Princess Maura

Iegani (character) – uncle to Empress Gitar, spiritual advisor to the Dinii, and founder of secret society that protects Princess Maura

Jezra (character) – first wife to Dorak, mother of his first child

Jon (character) – minister to Governor Petenptope of the northern Hasan Daegian state of Kinton

Kaseri (place) – name of the planet

Kaysia (place) – land in which Anqara was located

KiKu (character) – Zoar's Hetmaan, former prince of Hittal who becomes a double spy

KiKusan (character) – daughter of Kiku and concubine of Zoar

Kimtimee (character) – Queen Abisola's highest-ranking general

Kinton (place) – northern region of Hasan Daeg

Kittum (place) – country to the east of Hasan Daeg which has a treaty with Bhuttan

Knoxel (character) – magician who was mentor to Zedek

Land of the Setting Sun (place) – romantic name given to Hasan Daeg by the Bhuttanians

Lahor (place) – former island home of the Lahorians

Lahorians (characters) – originally from Lahor and ancient enemies of the Dinii

Madric (character) – KiKu's first wife

Mamora (character) – first wife of Zoar and sister of KiKu

Maura (character) – tenth ruler of Hasan Daeg, daughter of Queen Abisola and Consort Iasos

Meagan of Skujpor (character) – healer to the royal house of de Magela and member of the House of Magi

Mehmet (character) – high priestess of the House of Magi

Mekonia (character) – nature goddess of the Hasan Daegians

MeNe (character) – Yesemek's first lieutenant

Mikkotto (character) – Hasan Daegian baroness who becomes a traitor and joins with Zoar

Mingo tree – tree with large, flat limbs that is treasured for its endurance, beauty, and strength

Mother Bogazkoy/Royal Bogazkoy – intelligent, self-aware plants that have a special relationship with Hasan Daegian rulers

Nani (character) – adopted granddaughter of Lady Sari

Noabini (character) – Mehmet's assistant who becomes high priestess of the House of Magi

O Konya (place) – capital of Hasan Daeg

Onxor (character) – priest of Bhuttu

Pearl (character) – second wife of KiKu and a healer

Petenptope (character) – governor of the northern Hasan Daegian province of Kinton

Plain of Moab (place) – traditional home of nomadic people

Prosperot (character) – one of two top Bhuttanian generals, along with Alexanee

Qatou (place) – Hasan Daegian city

Rakel (character) – Lahorian woman who helps Princess Maura

Red – royal color of the Bhuttanians

Renna (character) – daughter of Riza

Riza (character) – scion from oldest noble family in Hasan Daeg

Rooshars – rare marsh flower

Rosalind (character) – first queen of Hasan Daeg

Royal Bogazkoy – plant offspring of the Mother Bogazkoy

Rubank (character) – consul to Queen Abisola and then to Queen Maura

Sari (character) – Hasan Daegian nurse to Queen Maura/Queen Abisola and grandmother of Mikkotto and Nani

Shaybar – Bhuttanian drink of boiled water or milk mixed with an equal portion of borax blood

Siddig (character) – Bhuttanian healer who helped Timon

Sinjo – rare berry made into wine that stimulates feelings of pleasure

Siva (place) – desert country south of Hasan Daeg

Sivans (characters) – merchant desert people

Sumsumitoyo (character) – family name of Mikkotto and Sari

Tarsus (character) – gray male hawk Dini who belongs to secret society that protects Maura

Tippa/Tippu (characters) – third and fourth twin wives of KiKu, artists

Tnpothar (character) – Zoar's father

Toppo (character) – red female hawk Dini, belongs to the secret society that protects Maura

Tsnsuni – ritualistic national prayer for the Hasan Daegian queen

Uultepes – mythical animals that are the symbol of Hasan Daegian royalty

Water Orbs – Lahorian mechanical devices constructed for transportation

Wise Ones (character) – title for the Lahorians

Yagomba tree – largest hardwood tree on Kaseri, has mystical powers

Yappor (place) – sacred lake of the Hasan Daegians and thought to be home of their goddess, Mekonia; home to the Lahorians

Yesemek (character) – commander-in-chief of the Dinii and wife to Iegani

Yeti (character) – red female hawk Dini, belongs to secret society that protects Maura

Yubuto (character) – sacrificed son of Mikkotto

Zedek (character) – Black Cacodemon's given name

Zoar (character) – aga (king) of the Bhuttanians

Wall Of Conquest

Preface

Centuries ago, the Dinii, Overlords of the planet Kaseri, were defeated by the Lahorians, an advanced race from the sea islands of Lahore.

Despondent, the Dinii retreated to Hasan Daeg. Unable to care for their slaves, they released them from bondage while continuing to watch over them in secret.

Believing they had been abandoned by their former masters, the Hasan Daegians developed into a prosperous agricultural society, having all but forgotten their origins. For two thousand years, they thrived in Hasan Daeg, by retreating from the rest of the world and emerging into a pacifist society. Hiding behind a wall of hypnotic mist, they considered their world secure from outside influences.

Unknown to the Hasan Daegians—Zoar, the powerful Aga of Bhuttan, arose in the east. His most burning desire was to become Overlord of Kaseri. His policies of conquering and plundering threatened to transform Kaseri into a wasteland, never to recover.

The Lahorians, threatened by Zoar's marauding, emerged from their underwater retreat to contact their former enemies, the Dinii. Able to see into the future, the Lahorians persuaded the Dinii to again establish relations with the ruling Hasan Daeg family to counter the threat from Zoar.

The Lahorians instructed the Dinii to take the Hasan Daegian queen's only heir, Princess Maura, and raise her as a warrior, who could defeat Zoar, thus allowing the Lahorians to continue their evolution into pure energy.

At eighteen, the young Maura, commanding a combined army of Hasan Daegians, Dinii, Anqarians, and mercenaries, won the first battle against Zoar's more experienced Bhuttanian army, but total capitulation of the Bhuttanians eluded her grasp.

Dorak, Zoar's son, succeeded upon his father's death and now the Aga of Bhuttan, realized he would be unable to defeat Princess Maura unless he used magic. He called forth the Black Cacodemon, an evil wizard.

With aid of the dark arts, Dorak won the war and conquered Hasan Daeg, banishing the Dinii.

Desirous of the Hasan Daegian throne and wishing the people to see his rule as legitimate, Dorak connived to marry Maura. Unexpectedly, he fell in love with her, but his ambition overshadowed his love.

Maura grew to love Dorak but remained wary of

him. Realizing she could never influence Dorak regardless of their feelings for each other, Maura fled. She escaped and fled to Atetelco, the ancient capital of the Dinii. There she underwent a "mating ritual" with the Mother Bogazkoy, a primeval sentient tree with the ability to impart mysterious powers.

The Black Cacodemon, Dorak's malevolent wizard, learned of the Mother Bogazkoy's power. Betraying Dorak, he hastened to Atetelco and discovered Maura deep inside the Bogazkoy's secret lair.

To save Maura, Dorak followed, but during the confrontation, the wizard cast a spell, sending Dorak into a dark netherworld. Maura battled the Black Cacodemon and destroyed him.

Grief-stricken, Maura fell into despair until a mysterious apparition appeared and came to her aid. The spirit of Queen Rosalind, the first ruler of Hasan Daeg, led Maura to a secret throne room where Rosalind's bones had been in repose for centuries.

Our last story ended with Maura seated on the ancient throne of Rosalind, awaiting the arrival of Dorak's troops.

Thus our new adventure begins.

1

Maura de Magela looked unhappy.

This pleased Timon not one bit, but he could say nothing until his master, the Consul Rubank, whose palanquin he trudged alongside, beckoned.

The empress tapped her fingers impatiently on the arm of her carved throne made from bones of those vanquished by previous Bhuttanian rulers—and by her as well. The empress had anyone who opposed her leadership executed, including Hasan Daegians.

The throne sat upon a carved wooden dais, decorated with Imperial flags and resting upon a massive painted wagon pulled by a team of festive borax wearing plumed headgear. A detachable canopy of rare wood carved with images of dragons and other Bhuttanian symbols covered the rolling platform.

One had to be alert not to stumble under it and be

crushed for it could not stop in haste.

The empress motioned to her consul who waved for the wagon to stop.

Timon, who acted as Rubank's scribe, kneeled as did others.

Fanning herself, the empress stepped down onto the dusty ground.

The young scribe did not like having close contact with the empress. She frightened him with her blue skin and fierce expressions. Her mercurial moods were such that he always waited for a calamity to fall. Timon wished he had remained a nameless scribe in the guild for he despised his duties as royal scribe, but Rubank had handpicked him.

If Empress Maura noticed Timon's discomfort, she did not show it.

They were on their way to Bhuttan so she could officially assume the reins of government in the capital city of Bhuttani. She was the mother of Princess Dyanna, heir to the throne of the Bhuttanian Empire, and would rule as Dowager Regent until the child became of age.

Timon chuckled when he thought of the empress relinquishing power she had ruthlessly fought to gain. He doubted she would voluntarily turn over control when the time came for the child to ascend to the throne.

Get out your tablets, commanded Rubank with the sign language Timon had devised for the consul to communicate with him.

Previously, Timon had to guess what the consul wanted or wait for him to write his instructions down. Timon's thoughts that a tongueless advisor to a ruler benefited no one and Rubank was too old to be of any real use were kept to himself.

How many times do I have to tell you that you must be ready for the empress at all times! Rubank loved his new way of communicating and was quite adept at it.

Timon shook his head. He regretted that he had designed the hand language, for Rubank never shut up now.

As Timon unwrapped moist clay tablets from his leather pouch, two uultepes jumped off the royal platform with singular grace. The great beasts, conjured by magic, constantly stayed near the side of the empress. One pressed close to Timon, knocking him down. It circled, taking care to look Timon in the eye.

The strong odor of the brindle animals mingled with the dust of the marching army caused Timon to erupt in a fit of coughing. He brought his fist to his mouth, hoping to stifle the hack rising from his chest. He glanced up red-faced to see if the empress had noticed his breach of protocol.

She had not.

Timon immediately stood up, and grabbed his tablet and stylus, ignoring the snickers of the guards, who watched as the uultepes circled again pressing even closer. Timon, ready this time, took the sharp end of his wooden stylus and stabbed a paw of one of the giant cats.

The uultepe's eyes widened. Angry, it trotted toward its mistress after giving Timon a malevolent glance.

Timon smiled. Brushing off his dusty knees with several quiet groans, he reluctantly followed. Timon made a mental note to speak to Rubank about a transfer again as he stumbled along. Fumbling with his stylus and wet clay tablets, he dodged an army trudging in the opposite direction.

Scribes used beeswax, wood, and cloth, but clay tablets were preferred on a military march. The wet clay was never allowed to dry out and could be used over and over again.

Timon thought the heavy clay tablets a nuisance and hated working with them, but then Timon hated everything about his life at the moment. Oh, he longed to escape.

Empress Maura strode steadily toward the rear of the army with her hands clasped behind her back.

Two lads-in-waiting struggled to keep the costly

embroidered train of her light blue and gold gown out of the dirt.

Underneath the skirt of her gown, Timon could see leather boots and heavy, twined cotton pants commonly worn by most Bhuttanian soldiers. He was sure there would also be a dagger or two tucked away somewhere on her royal personage.

Timon was aware the empress only donned the beautiful gown to please the more conservative elements of her court. She wore the soldier's clothes to please herself. On a second's notice, she could rip the gown off, becoming a skilled combatant. She had become the deadliest woman in the Bhuttanian Empire, which no one could best, regardless of their proficiency with weapons.

There were others who were more dexterous in swinging an axe or lighter on their feet with a sword, but she possessed brute strength and lightning fast agility.

Perhaps a Dini possessed sufficient skill and strength to topple the empress, but the Dinii were seen no more.

The empress rested her eyes upon Timon, as she inclined her head. "What is the name of you, boy?"

Timon blinked and heard himself replying, "My name is Timon Ben Ibin Moab. My people are from the

Steppes of Moab named after the first of my ancestors." He bowed his head.

"We will cut through the Steppes of Moab before we reach Bhuttani."

Timon continued to stare at the ground. "Yes, Empress. My home is only a week or so from here."

"You have been in the consul's employment for how long?"

"Many moons."

He's unusually clever, Great Mother, Rubank wrote on a tablet for the empress. *He has an impressive talent for symbols and language.*

Maura considered this information for a moment after reading the tablet. "He must be, Consul, as I do not see your usual interpreters with you."

She addressed Timon directly. "Timon Ben Ibin Moab, you will come to my tent after the evening meal and show me from whence you came on my map," commanded the empress. She turned her head from the consul and the lowly scribe, who realized he had just wet himself.

Luckily, Timon's long woven tunic covered his disgrace. He touched his fingers to his heart and then his lips with a theatrical flourish. Seeing Rubank was displeased, Timon gave the usual Bhuttanian salute of the fist to his heart. With a wave of her hand, Maura dismissed both Rubank and Timon.

Timon reluctantly followed the silent Rubank and helped him into his palanquin. The years of war between the Bhuttanians and Hasan Daegians had strained the royal consul's heart. Rubank did little these days to be of real use to the empress except give her occasional advice.

Still, the empress showed Rubank respect by letting him keep his title and honors. In fact, Timon noticed she rarely let Rubank out of her sight.

Timon pinched the side of his face. *It is regarding things which are none of my business that got me noticed by the empress today!* thought Timon, but still he pondered the reasons why Maura de Magela, Dowager Regent, Aganess of the Bhuttanian Empire, Tenth Queen of Hasan Daeg, and Great Mother of Kaseri, might need an old man who was past his prime.

Timon had heard Rubank served Queen Abisola, Maura's mother, for much of her reign. *That would make him—let's see—past one hundred, maybe older,* Timon thought as he counted on his fingers. Timon shook his head in disbelief and hurried to catch up with Rubank's palanquin.

These Hasan Daegians lived a very long time.

2

The army followed the same routine.

Before dusk, the empress had her husband's favorite horse saddled and brought to her. With only the uultepes for company, she rode behind the main body of the army where she awaited scouts, who had been sent in search of stray feathers that might have fallen from the elusive Dinii.

Upon their return each day, she'd excitedly go through their pouches full of feathers with eager anticipation until she dropped the last feather in disappointment at finding no Dini feather.

"Maybe tomorrow," she murmured to the sweating couriers. "Go. Get something to eat." Empress Maura would then gaze at the distant horizon until darkness.

Timon was so bored with this daily scene, he thought he'd scream. To ease his frustration, he played games in his imagination, waiting for the empress to return to her wagon.

Sometimes, he looked at Rubank, imagining him dressed as a fool, complete with a purple face and a green nose. This would cause Timon to smile. Other times, he pictured the empress on her knees begging him to make love to her.

"Timon, why are you grinning?"

Timon's eyes widened as he realized the empress was standing before him speaking.

"Are you dim-witted?"

"No, Great Mother. My mind drifted off. A hundred pardons."

Maura's eyes narrowed as her jaw tightened. "That could be a foolish mistake, which might cost you your life, Royal Scribe."

Timon's face flushed. He bowed very low. "A thousand pardons. It will never happen again."

"I'm not talking about me causing you harm, boy. An assassin could make straight for me, and if you are not alert, you could fall right in her pathway. Death by mere association. Beware!" Grumbling to herself about Timon, the somber empress strode off on foot in haste.

One of the uultepes turned and snarled a warning before following her queen.

Timon mouthed an oath under his breath at the

uultepe. Struggling to hold his tablets and writing sticks, Timon hurried after the empress, dropping a stylus here and there.

Maura made way to her tent, which was hurriedly being prepared by many servants. Out of the corner of her eye, Maura saw flickering lights on the northern horizon as eventide approached.

No troops of hers were straggling in from that direction.

Maura speculated on who it might be and wondered how her scouts had failed to inform her of approaching strangers in the area.

All the local people had given their fealty to her, so she knew it was not an opposing force. "You there," she called to a Bhuttanian. "Help this boy up."

The soldier immediately ran over to Timon and intertwined his hands together. Timon clumsily swung a foot in the soldier's hands and climbed atop his shoulders, straining to get a look at the entourage approaching the army.

"What do you see?" called Maura.

"They ride Bhuttanian war steeds. There are numerous wagons as well, so there must be women and children, but their banners are too far away. I can't make them out." Timon jumped down with his pens spilling upon the ground. He thanked the embarrassed soldier helping to pick them up.

"Let's hurry to my tent. A courier awaits with news, I'm sure," she called to Timon.

"I hope so, or it will be someone's head," muttered Timon, breaking into a run.

As expected, an out-of-breath courier waited in the tent as the empress strode in.

"Is it an emergency?" she asked the courier.

The stalwart courier shook her head, struggling to regain her breath.

Maura smiled. "Good. You may tell me as I make ready for dinner."

The courier followed the empress into her private quarters.

Lads-in-waiting stood eagerly.

Maura washed her dusty face and hands. Grabbing a towel, she sat as one of her servants pulled off her boots and washed her feet. "What news do you have, woman?" Maura grunted as one of the servants tried to coax her unruly hair into a braid.

"Prince KiKu of Hittal humbly requests permission to enter the perimeter of Her Majesty's camp."

Timon shivered when he heard the name KiKu.

"KiKu! Here?" asked Maura as she reached back, grabbing the annoying comb out of the servant's hand and hurling it across the room.

Maura stood, and two servants immediately began unbuckling her pants and shirt. A beautiful pale green lounging gown with gold trousers was produced for her inspection. Pleased with the embroidered flower designs on the gown, she nodded yes. The empress stood with her arms extended. The servants removed her tunic and wiped down her arms, chest, and back. Stepping out of her trousers, her legs and buttocks were cleansed as well.

The lads, delighted the empress approved their selection, dressed her.

The courier stood at attention and stared at the tent wall, never looking at the empress.

Sensing the courier was embarrassed at being in the presence of the empress while dressing, Maura gave leave for the courier to retire.

Relieved, the courier backed out of the chamber while bowing.

Maura turned to Timon, who was kneeling in obeisance with his forehead pressed against a carpeted floor. "Ask Prince KiKu to join me for dinner this evening. Tonight, he will set his tents outside the perimeter, but tomorrow, he may place his tent next to mine."

Timon was about to remind the empress his guild only allowed him to write messages, not deliver them but thought better of it. He rose to his feet and bowed.

"Be early for dinner to take notes and work with my map," Maura ordered sharply as she rotated on her stool to face the blushing Bhuttanian.

Timon salaamed and backed out of the chamber. Once outside, Timon grimaced as he pondered how he could shuffle this duty onto someone else. He did not want to be around the infamous KiKu, let alone speak directly with him.

Obviously, no one else did, either.

He asked several officers, but they declined harshly, backing away from his annoying request.

Mustering his courage, Timon commandeered a pony cart with a servant holding a torch and trotted over to the dancing strobes of light from paper lanterns that signaled KiKu's rapid advance toward the Bhuttanian army.

While the empress was the most dangerous woman in the Empire, KiKu the Hetmaan was the most dangerous man in the Empire.

Timon hoped he would be able to recite the empress' message and leave.

One never knew with the renowned and loathsome KiKu.

One just never knew.

3

Maura sat on a high dais.

Along with Rubank and the High Priestess of Magi, Maura sat upright, sipping colla tea Hasan Daegian style. She listened politely to poetry offered by a minstrel, but when the singer began reciting about love, the empress waved her off. She would rather hear about epic deeds of long-ago heroes.

Love poetry only made Maura sad. She had lost both of her loves, Dorak and Chaun Maaun, and did not want to be reminded.

The minstrel strummed on her lyre while singing a ribald song about a countess and her stable boy.

The Hasan Daegian women of Maura's court thought the song amusing, but their husbands found it demeaning.

The Hasan Daegian males had fought hard to win

legal and social rights. They finally had a matriarch who was sympathetic to their plight, and they disliked anything that detracted from their honors won fighting the last war, where they had made bold strides toward equality with women. The Hasan Daegian males studied the empress with interest.

Her eyes narrowed.

Many of the Hasan Daegian men turned their heads, so their wives could not see their smiles of relief at their ruler's displeasure. As Maura's eyes grew bright with anger, the men relaxed and leaned back in their chairs. Some even snickered at a particular verse. If the men hadn't had so much to lose, they might have thought the song was funny as well.

The minstrel, sensing the empress was not interested in her choice again, switched to peasant tunes she had learned from the Bhuttanians.

The Bhuttanians had no talent for art or music. Their songs tended to be uncomplicated, repetitive verses that demanded a call and response accompanied by a drum. But these songs would do until the minstrel could think of something else. As it turned out, she didn't have time.

The great gong sounded.

The minstrel was quickly escorted away.

The ancient Keeper Of The Palace waited for every-one to become quiet. It did not take long. "Great

Mother," she boomed with her loud, steady voice. "Prince KiKu of Hittal asks permission to enter."

Maura nodded.

The High Priestess of Magi and Rubank rose to meet Prince KiKu, the famous spy who had helped topple the mighty Aga Zoar.

The Bhuttanians, after glancing at General Alexanee who gave a signal, also rose. They refrained from spitting on the spylord, who had betrayed their aga, though mutters and oaths could be heard throughout the tent.

"I can't believe he would show his face here."

"I hope for his sake he doesn't sleep too soundly."

"May all his children see a painful death before his old age."

"He should be skinned alive."

"May his son sleep with his mother and his wife sleep with a borax."

Timon, who was sitting below the royal dais, could feel the electric charge in the air. He tucked his feet under his gown. For once, there was going to be excitement on this dreary march, and he was not going to miss it.

The High Priestess, overhearing some of the remarks, thought it folly for the empress to receive Prince KiKu publicly. Did the empress not realize the Bhuttanians hated KiKu, and their hatred of anyone always ran white-hot? She chanced a glance at Maura.

The face of the empress remained as impassive as carved stone.

The flap of the great tent opened. A tall, wiry man stepped forward into the smoke-filled pavilion of the empress.

Timon held his breath. Although he had delivered the empress' message, he had only seen a shadowy figure, who turned his face away. Timon was relieved that the spylord had taken no interest in him. The man had said nothing until Timon got the idea he should leave, which he did with haste. Timon scratched his chin in surprise. Now the great KiKu was before him, and he was as tall as any Bhuttanian.

Prince KiKu had harsh, black eyes, which darted about quickly. He sensed the hatred of the Bhuttanians. KiKu stifled a laugh. For years he had served the dreaded Zoar while watching his sister disintegrate under her marriage to him. Sweating and toiling under the hateful Bhuttanian yoke, KiKu was able to throw it off. Now he stood before the most powerful woman on Kaseri, who ruled over the despised Bhuttanians, his sworn enemies. It gave him great pleasure that she was not even Bhuttanian.

And the empress liked him—was even beholden to him. No Bhuttanian dared touch him on pain of losing his head. KiKu chuckled to himself. This afforded him better security than having a hundred guards. Abject fear had its uses.

Followed by four women, KiKu strode toward the dais. His eyes fell upon some familiar faces. He remembered Rubank, a senior advisor to Maura's mother, Queen Abisola. KiKu was surprised at how Rubank had aged in the two years since he had last seen him. Recognizing the indigo robes of the High Priestess of Magi, he did not know the face. He would think about her later. Out of the corner of his eye, he spied General Alexanee. He would have to watch that one carefully.

Finally, he looked upon Maura herself, feeling heat rising from her skin. It was like the sun's summer warmth.

The empress radiated a blue glow while emitting pale beams of gold and pink light from her hands and head. The power of the Mother Bogazkoy had not deserted her. The empress seemed a goddess. No wonder the Bhuttanians followed her.

KiKu breathed out slowly.

SHE MUST HAVE THE BOGAZKOY WITH HER!

The former hetmaan halted before the dais and knelt in keeping with Bhuttanian custom, folding his lush burgundy gown beneath him. "Greetings, Great

Mother," he called out.

"Greetings, Prince KiKu of Hittal. Rise. I wish to see your face." Maura waved her fan impatiently while KiKu struggled to his feet. "I see you have acquired bad knees, Lord KiKu."

KiKu motioned to one of his companions to help him. "Old age, Great Mother."

"As well as too much rich food and wine," replied Maura, referring to KiKu's little potbelly.

Twitters arose among the court.

KiKu spoke quickly. "The gods have been good to me, Great Mother."

"What wind blows you here?"

"I have longed for the companionship of my empress and ruling lady. I wish only to bask in your infinite glory."

"As if there were any truth in those words, but never mind. May we be introduced?" the empress asked, pointing to the women standing behind KiKu.

"Great Mother, may I present my wives?"

Maura snapped open her fan, which meant approval in Hasan Daeg.

KiKu gestured to the oldest of the group.

A middle-aged woman stepped forward, looking frightened. Her eyes seemed to bolt everywhere, but one could sense a keen intelligence behind her plain face. The woman offered a silver box. Gently laying it on the first step of the dais, the woman spoke. "Great Mother, my name is Madric. I was taken prisoner seven years ago and sent to work as a tutor for a wealthy Camaroon in the Bhuttanian district of Zipei until I was liberated. I wish to present a token of gratitude for my release and reunion with my family." She stepped back.

One of the guards made her way to retrieve the box until the empress stopped her. "I'm sure it will give Madric great pleasure to open the box herself," purred Maura.

KiKu's face gave a faint impression of a smile. He had taught Maura well.

Death could easily be delivered in the guise of a gift by a friend. Madric stepped forward again and quickly gathered the silver box. With deft fingers, she undid a tiny silver clasp. "Great Mother, I present precious amber from my homeland."

She turned the box over, and large pieces of yellow amber tumbled onto the carpeted steps of the dais. "Purported to heal certain illnesses, amber can also be used in magic. It is my deepest hope that my humble gift will be acceptable to the woman who set me free from the terrible, dark place in which I had lived for so many years."

"It was not just I who has set you free, Madric,"

replied the empress. "Thousands have sacrificed so the yoke of tyranny could be thrown off."

The faces of the Bhuttanian officers grew dark at the implied insult to their former ruler but said nothing.

"Your gift will be accepted. I need earrings for my daughter. A small portion of this beautiful amber will do nicely."

Madric beamed at the suggestion that her amber would be used as jewelry for Princess Dyanna. She stepped back to her place behind KiKu.

KiKu motioned for another wife to approach the dais.

A woman in her late thirties with rough-looking hands offered a large leather bag. Opening it, she exposed hundreds of small vials filled with colored liquids. "My name is Pearl. I am a healer from the Qiowa river region. My specialty is fevers. I was taken five years ago from the city of Peygen and forced to work in Bhuttan. I first worked as a servant in the house of one of the officers who raided my home. A pox, unknown to me, overtook the city in which I had been placed. The wife and daughter of the officer to whom I belonged contracted the illness. I saved them, but the wife still sent me away as her husband began to love me. I then worked as a common laborer in the fields." She smiled briefly, revealing several missing teeth. "I

escaped and made my way to Hittal where I met Prince
KiKu. He honored me by marrying a poor one such as
I."

Pointing to the vials, Pearl continued, "These are all
the ointments and oils I use in the treatment of my
patients. I give them to you to add to your medical
knowledge." She handed a servant a scroll. "This is to
be kept with the vials. It contains all the information
needed to use them." Pearl bowed and returned to her
place in KiKu's retinue.

The empress remained silent.

KiKu wondered if the empress was displeased with
his wife's gift.

The empress spoke. "I am sure I speak on behalf of
our learned physicians when I say your gift is most
precious and generous. I thank you from the bottom of
my heart."

Pearl's face lit up.

Though KiKu's face remained unreadable, he felt
relieved. The gifts of his wives were accepted with much
honor. KiKu was sure he had not lost favor with the
empress. He motioned for the last two remaining wives.
They were of similar stature and looks.

The empress surmised they were sisters and the
youngest of the wives.

They bowed graciously, and one could see they were

suppressing giggles behind their pretty pink mouths.

The empress was slightly amused.

"I am Tippu," announced one of the girls. "This is my twin, Tippa. We are distant cousins of Prince KiKu. Most of our family died during the great famine. Prince KiKu found us and took us in. We are here to present you with a token of our esteem."

They laid down the heavy object they had been carrying and pulled off the shimmering cloth covering it. "We are artists, and we carved this out of obsidian."

The empress leaned forward to observe the statue. "May I ask the interpretation of this piece?"

Tippu's face flushed. "The woman in the carving represents you, Great Mother. At her breasts are two starving children suckling. The children represent—well," claimed Tippu, waving her hand at the congregation, "US!"

Maura had a servant bring the statue to her so she could touch it. "Again, I am delighted with a gift presented to me by the wives of an old comrade." She patted the statue. "I will take this with me all the way to Bhuttani, and place it in the official gardens of the aga's palace, where it will remain for the pleasure of all agas to come after me."

She turned to KiKu. "Thank you, Prince KiKu. Couches have been prepared for you. Ask anything you need for your comfort, and it will be given to you."

Timon smiled to himself as he watched KiKu being led away.

Not even the empress dared to incur the wrath of the Bhuttanian nobles by asking the traitor to dine on the dais with her.

Prince KiKu bowed, his face reflecting nothing of displeasure. KiKu followed a servant who made room for him near the Hasan Daegians and away from the hostile glares of the Bhuttanians. As he turned, KiKu met Timon's stare. His eyes, unsettled at the sight of Timon, did not betray recognition of the young scribe.

Timon gave a start and looked away. Composing himself quickly, Timon lifted his eyes to confront the infamous man, but KiKu was already escorting his wives to their couches. Timon felt his heart pounding in his chest as he watched the former spylord approach his old comrades.

It did not go unnoticed by the Bhuttanians that all of the Hasan Daegians stood as KiKu had made his way toward them. To the Bhuttanians, he was a traitorous servant of their former aga.

To the Hasan Daegians, he was an honored servant of their people.

Such was the business of war.

Sooner or later, one of the Bhuttanians would kill

him, but not tonight with the Imperial Guards watching. The Bhuttanians turned their heads and resumed eating their meals. They were doubtful that KiKu would be alive for much longer.

4

The gangly scribe waited.

Timon stood with a little knot of impatient men wishing to petition the empress. He usually sat behind the empress, alongside Rubank, during court, but as the empress had invited him, he was to be treated as a guest. The wait gave Timon ample opportunity to study the proceedings without being noticed. Typically, all he saw was the back of the empress' head or the floor, as he could not directly gaze upon Maura. He missed all the subtleties of body movement and eye contact. And he was so busy translating for Rubank and waiting for the consul's responses, he missed the inflections of voice. He could now study the expressions and countenance of his betters.

He noted Maura cut an impressive figure sitting on her throne of bones, fixed on a rough-hewn dais covered with mats woven with intricate designs from Hasan Daeg.

Yellow flowers were interwoven into the braids of Maura's black-blue hair with its one lock of snow white at her widow's peak. Although her bearing was regal, Timon observed Maura's features to be average. She offered a severe expression with her blue-tinted eyes and their darker blue orbs, making her face resemble a mask. One could only guess what she truly thought.

Timon glanced about for KiKu. He was nowhere to be seen. The empress had not invited him to court. Timon tucked this information comfortably in his mind. He would retrieve it later when he could study the day's events in private.

On a lower level of the dais sat the High Priestess of the House of Magi with several other priestesses in their severe, dark blue-green robes. With their hands folded, they sat silently while their expressive eyes darted back and forth, surveying all things around them. Once in a great while, an older priestess dozed off for a few moments, but that was rare.

It was Timon's contention this was a ploy to put people off-guard. He was puzzled, as he could never discern the women's true purpose. They rarely advised the empress, and none of the information they collected was ever shared with the military or other advisors.

They spent most of their time scribbling in huge books, cataloging everything they saw and heard on their journey to Bhuttan. He thought them a waste of the empire's money.

Behind the empress, on her right, was Rubank sitting with one leg on a small stool. He had problems with gout and had been placed on a strict diet by the royal physician. Rubank was the last of the older Hasan Daegian advisors who had survived the Great War, except for the fabled KiKu.

Surrounding this tight little group languished various military advisors and generals, both Hasan Daegian and Bhuttanian. They stood with their countrymen according to rank and did little to interact with each other.

The empress had forbidden fighting between Hasan Daegians and Bhuttanians, showing no partiality when sentencing to death those who disobeyed. So the former enemies had as little to do with each other as possible. They talked with their backs turned, chatting intimately among themselves reviewing the day's events.

Timon took in all of the little dramas of court. He found Rubank, as all Hasan Daegians, to be vain about his appearance.

The Hasan Daegians seemed an even-tempered people with occasional bouts of excitability when confronted with small, irritating matters such as a lack of clean water for baths. He thought their obsession with cleanliness to be ridiculous, though he had to admit the Hasan Daegians seemed to be sick less often than their Bhuttanian counterparts—and certainly smelled better.

Timon felt the hair on the back of his neck rise. He suddenly realized the empress was watching him observe the court. He forced his eyes up to the dais and met hers quickly. He salaamed by pressing his right palm against his forehead and lowered his eyes, but not before he saw her motion to one of her guards.

He waited obediently until the guard fetched him and brought him before the empress. Timon bowed very low, keeping his head pressed to the ground until the empress gave him permission to look up.

"I see you are wearing a new robe, Master Timon," commented the empress, studying his tunic's fabric.

Timon blushed, not knowing how to reply. It embarrassed him that the empress took notice of what he wore. He could feel Rubank's worried eyes upon him and hoped he had not shamed his benefactor. It would only mean trouble for him later. Timon pointed to the detailed borax design embossed on the front of his robe, stammering, "Uh, this work is done by the women in my mother's village. They take great pride in their workmanship."

"Pray, tell me, where is your mother's village, good scribe?"

"My mother is from a remote village on the Plain of Moab. Less than four hundred people live there."

Maura leaned back and considered the young man standing before her. Tall and gaunt with spindly arms, Timon was anything but a soldier, only he was too young to realize it. She knew he dreamt of glory and chafed under his current position. Maura also knew he would be killed within minutes on the battlefield. Timon was so lacking the skills of a warrior that Maura could lean across the space that divided them and crush his throat with her bare hands before he realized what was happening to him.

The empress blinked and unclenched her hands. She motioned to a nearby servant, who spread out an old map. "Show me your homeland," she commanded Timon. "You may sit," she added as a servant brought a small stool.

The thin scribe blanched, leaning over the map. It was a detailed depiction of the known world drawn on animal parchment.

Timon's eyes followed the lines of the mountains to the rivers, which flowed near his home. He could not fathom why the empress would be interested in his tiny village. "It is here," he lied.

"Tell me about your homeland."

"What shall I tell you, Great Mother?"

"Anything. What did you do as a child? Do you love your mother? Who owns the spoons in the houses—the men or the women? Who is the most respected person in the village and why? Anything. Anything at all."

A thoughtful servant handed Timon a drink, and he took a sip while collecting his thoughts. "My people are nomadic. In the summer, we travel to the base of the mountains with our horses and grazing animals. There we live in small tents made of felt and leather. During the winter, we travel down to the steppes and live in houses made of stone." He looked at the empress.

She was quiet.

"Pray, continue," chimed in the High Priestess from the House of Magi.

When the empress did not stir, he continued. "I am the baby in my family with two elder sisters. I used to see them every summer when they came to the mountains. We do not speak of personal things, as it is not allowed between unmarried men and women. I do not know what the lives of my sisters have been like or how they feel."

"Very interesting," commented the High Priestess.

"What is, High Priestess?" Timon asked.

"The fact there is no personal conversation between the sexes."

"As I have explained, we are a simple people. Our needs are few. There is not much to discuss besides the weather and our livestock." Timon twisted uneasily and added, "There is no need for us to talk. It only leads to trouble."

"How is that?" asked the High Priestess.

"Forbidden feelings. Taboo."

The High Priestess rebutted, "My young man, one does not need conversation for love if that is what you are referring to. One only needs to behold another person. To connect in the eyes to connect in the heart." She studied him, trying to discern his age. She smiled thoughtfully. "You are too young to understand. Continue with other matters. How were you brought here?"

"When Zoar came through our region on his way to Hasan Daeg, I joined his army." Timon added quickly, "I worked with the horses until my superior noticed I had an aptitude for symbols and numbers." Timon sat up proudly upon his stool. "I have a way with words— written, of course—and I picked up the language easily once in Hasan Daeg."

"Zoar was searching for people who had a head for symbols?" asked Maura, scowling at the bottom of an empty glass. It was immediately filled with colla tea.

"Yes, Great Mother. He was searching for these

kinds of people. I was treated well and given lots to eat even though I trained many hours a day. I stayed in the ranks of the scribes until the royal consul sought me out and brought me thus."

"But you are not a true Bhuttanian," stated the empress, studying Timon's expression.

Timon's face grew red, and he blustered, "I am Bhuttanian, Great Mother!"

The Hasan Daegians noticed the Bhuttanians watched the royal party intently. The entire tent grew quiet except for the bustling noises the servants made.

The High Priestess said, "No offense was intended, Royal Scribe. The empress only meant to clarify that the Moabites were absorbed by the Bhuttanian Empire before Aga Tnpothar's reign. According to oral history, the Moabites were a nomadic people akin to the Bhuttanians. They did not worship Bhuttu or Bhutta, but only one god who has no name. When the Moabites did not pay their annual tribute one spring, the Bhuttanians made war upon them. I make this comment because people of similar stock worship similar gods. Your people's god is much like that of the Anqarians— a god who is neither he nor she and has no name. It is only fodder for the mind."

Timon stiffened. He had made a terrible blunder before the empress by expressing umbrage at her words.

Timon's mind swirled with avenues of protocol to ease him out of this difficult situation, but he could not choose one. He slid off his stool and lowered himself before the empress, who studied him without expression. "Great Mother, please excuse my outburst! I spoke without thinking. You did not offend me. I am unused to being in such close proximity to your person in direct conversation. It caused me to be nervous and err like the peasant that I am."

"Rise, Timon. I take no issue with you. I wish to hear more of your country," replied the empress without rancor.

Alexanee, the highest-ranking Bhuttanian general, approached the royal dais. "Great Mother, may I speak on this matter?"

Maura nodded, curious that Alexanee involved himself. She waved Timon back onto his stool and motioned with her fan for another one to be brought for the general.

Alexanee had a recent leg injury, which had not yet healed, and was grateful. "Great Mother, my mother's grandfather fought in the campaign to chastise the Moabites. There was only one great battle. As the Moabites were herdsmen, we quickly overtook them and placed our own man in their tent."

"Do you consider his people to be Bhuttanian?" asked the High Priestess.

"It is said the Moabites and the Bhuttanians were one people many years ago, but that overpopulation caused the tribe to split and go their separate ways. If we are not from the same fathers, then we are very close cousins." Alexanee turned toward Timon and pointed. "Notice the high cheekbones. The same ruddy, dark skin. He is a tall man like every Bhuttanian male." Alexanee grinned. "Not yet filled out, but he soon will be if the gods are kind."

The High Priestess spoke, "It is true these are hallmarks of Bhuttanian bloodlines."

The empress nodded thoughtfully and stroked the amulet around her neck.

Timon spied the amulet conspicuously, as did everyone else when she touched it. It was rumored the necklace had belonged to the Black Cacodemon Zedek, who used it for his most powerful spells. Many whispered that the amulet produced magic from other worlds if one had the courage to use it.

"Tell me about your god," Maura commanded softly as she motioned for the musicians to play.

The musicians bowed and obliged by softly playing sad Hasan Daegian love songs.

The empress frowned at their selection.

The musicians quickly changed to a more upbeat tempo.

"It is just as I told you, Great Mother. Our god has no name."

"What powers does your god possess?"

Timon shrugged his shoulders. "One cannot say. Perhaps none, perhaps infinite."

"Where does your god live?" asked the empress.

"Legend has our god living in a lake on the steppes, but we have never seen it. It is only a rumor."

"Is your god male or female?" asked the High Priestess, rearranging her skirts.

Timon looked baffled. "I do not know." He paused for a moment. "I would say our god is neither, yet both."

"Did life begin with your god?" asked Maura.

"Yes, Great Mother."

Maura stated, "Then your god must be female."

"But one cannot deny that the spark of life begins with the male, Great Mother," pointed out the High Priestess.

Maura pondered for a moment. "Having a female goddess makes the most sense, but this boy says his god may be both."

"An oddity perhaps," murmured the High Priestess.

"No," said Timon, shaking his head. "It—he—she is everything. We are part of it. We are one."

Maura straightened up, as did the High Priestess.

The other priestesses began writing in their journals. "What did you say, Royal Scribe?"

Timon timidly looked at the tall and imposing empress sitting erect and stroking the huge uultepes lounging beside her with their eyes closed. "We are one."

"Why did you say that?"

"I—I don't know," stammered Timon. "It is something I have heard since my childhood."

"You have no priests or interpreters of your god, do you? No intermediaries?"

"Great Mother, we interpret for ourselves. We are one with this god; therefore, we listen to the god within us."

The empress leaned forward in her chair. "Tell me, Royal Scribe—and take care—do you feel your peoples' deaths without warning?"

One of the uultepes opened an eye and fixed it upon Timon, now squirming upon his stool.

"I feel sorry for anyone's death."

"No, no, no," scolded the empress, frustrated. "If a cousin of yours died, let's say, in a distant land, and you had no word, would you know she had died?"

Timon shook his head, seemingly confused at the question.

Maura sighed and fell back into her chair. Ever since

she had heard of the Moabites and their strange god who lived in a lake, she wanted to get close to a Moabite and learn all she could.

Timon would do.

She could see she was frightening the young man, and decided she would let him retire from the dais to sit with the pretty girls who waited on the High Priestesses. Only Hasan Daegian male virgins and older widowed noblewomen waited on the empress. "You may go," she said, waving her hand in dismissal.

Wrung out, Timon was only too happy to escape the piercing glare of the empress. He bowed very low before the empress and salaamed gracefully.

Maura took no notice, as she was deep in thought. Suddenly feeling weary, the empress stood. Her uultepes immediately followed, yawning and stretching. One of them playfully swatted at the High Priestess.

She turned disdainfully, slapping the big cat on the end of its nose.

Maura did not reprimand her as the uultepes tended to rip, bite, eat, tear, or gnaw anything they could find. She did not blame the High Priestess for taking issue with her bodyguards. She did not even understand their presence, though she had called them forth from the Mother Bogazkoy's secret chamber, guarding the remains of the beloved first Hasan Daegian queen, Rosalind.

Everyone rose to their feet. Bowing, they bid their empress good night. Though Maura had adopted many Bhuttanian customs, she did not like to sleep on couches in the middle of a tent with others, as had the former agas. She retired to her private chambers where a soothing bath and her lover for the evening awaited. The same person rarely entertained her twice, but mostly, she sent them away after questioning them about their lives.

Tonight, though, she wanted to feel the pressure of hands on her flesh, have sweet words whispered into her ear, and enjoy cool lips on her neck. Maura entered her private bedchamber and smiled salaciously at the man who waited for her. Perched precariously on a chair, he appeared nervous.

She had chosen a Bhuttanian who had been a high-ranking official under her husband, Dorak. He was a tall and rough-looking man with several wide scars across his face. The Bhuttanian seemed jittery and at a loss for what to say. He asked Maura if her day had gone well.

Astonished, Maura regarded him. "Do you care if my day went well?"

The Bhuttanian shrugged his shoulders, not knowing what else to say. "I thought it might ease the strain if you talked about your day," he answered sincerely.

"Do you think I have tiresome days like other people?

Like you, for instance?" she asked sarcastically.

"Of course, Great Mother," he replied, using the Hasan Daegian salutation. "You more than anyone." He paused for a moment. "Have I offended you, Great Mother? Perhaps I was at fault in comparing you to mere mortals?"

Maura went over to the Bhuttanian and stood before him. "Am I not like other mortals? What is the talk in the camp?"

Hesitating, the Bhuttanian finally peered into the empress' eyes. "They say you were once mortal, but you have mated with a devil tree, and now you are like one of the gods."

Maura gave a small laugh. She curtly dismissed her servants and poured her lover a cup of wine. Handing the cup to the man, she asked softly, "Does the fact that I may not be mortal frighten you?"

Happy that his hand did not shake, the lover revealed his tumultuous thoughts. Thinking he could not deceive her, he told the truth. "It frightens me very much, Great Lady. I do not know why you bothered to choose me. I am not young anymore." He shook his head in wonder and felt his face. "In fact, my countenance has little to admire. My wealth has been taken from me by misfortune. I have nothing to offer a queen, not even a gift such as a trinket."

"I think you have much to offer."

The Bhuttanian squared back his shoulders. "Though poor and broken, I will give what I can."

"Then I ask this of you. Make love to me as though I were a normal woman, one whom you desired." Maura felt the heat rise to her cheeks. "Can you do this for one night? I'll not ask more of you." She took the Bhuttanian's large, battered hands and pressed them to her breasts.

Realizing the empress might be lonely, the Bhuttanian took pity on her. "This I can do." He tried to hold her. "If only you will tell me how."

Seeing his stricken face, Maura laughed.

The Bhuttanian relaxed and laughed along with her.

She leaned forward, kissing him passionately.

He responded in kind and, picking her up, carried Maura to the bed.

"You will not find me ungrateful," Maura whispered. "In the morning, your property and more will be returned to you once you have pledged your loyalty to me."

The Bhuttanian lowered the empress on the soft bed. He was flushed with desire.

"I have one more request of you," said Maura.

"Ask, my lady, and if it is in my power, it is yours."

Maura looked deeply into his battered, questioning face. "Do not be gentle."

5

Maura climbed out of bed.

She donned nothing but Zedek's necklace. Touching the center of the amulet, she slipped behind her guards, going out the servant's entrance. Past dying fires and sleeping men, she sauntered unconcerned if one of them should awake. It mattered not for they would not be able to see her. She was invisible and would remain so for several minutes, the time needed to enter KiKu's chamber. She thought her entrance to KiKu's chamber easy until she saw the hetmaan sitting in a chair with only a small oil lamp casting a faint, warm glow about the tent.

KiKu gestured for Maura to approach when her unseen hand opened the flap to his private chambers.

Maura wrapped a blanket around herself and sat on a stool.

KiKu waited, seemingly undisturbed that an unseen force had entered his sleeping room. Finally, the spy could see faint features of Maura's face in the flickering of the oil lamp as she slowly became visible again. Her face was severe.

He waited for Maura to speak.

"Why are you here, KiKu?" she asked.

"I went back to my country, but there was no country to be found. The land was there, but my people had been scattered across the wastelands of Kaseri. Most of them are dead. The multitudes who have taken over my country are refugees from other places, and bitter ones at that. They have their own king and do not wish a Hittal to rule them. I have no army to force them." He paused.

"Is it my army you want?"

"For what purpose? To conquer a people who will always be in constant rebellion after your forces leave? I must face facts. They don't want me. They don't know the Hittal ways. It would be futile."

"Then why are you here amongst your deadliest enemies?"

He leaned toward Maura and whispered in her ear. "I have news that will interest you."

Dancing shadows thrown by the small oil lamp flickered across Maura's face.

KiKu thought her face was both cruel and beautiful, but it was her eyes that spoke the most to him.

Maura could not hide the longing in her blue eyes. KiKu knew she wanted Dorak still. Not even death could spoil her love for him. "Speak! Speak before I lose all manner of patience with you," she hissed.

"The Dinii have been seen!"

Maura grabbed KiKu's arm and squeezed.

KiKu patted her hand while trying to coax her constricting fingers from around his pained flesh. "Maura, you are cutting off my blood," he said, using her personal name.

Maura immediately withdrew her hand. She lowered her head to her chest, trying to dispel the anguish rising from her bowels. "Tell me quickly," she begged.

"I have heard strange rumors from among the priests of Bhuttu. Strange bird-like creatures have appeared before several priests as apparitions begging for release at the great temple in Bhuttani."

"Release from what?" Maura pressed her hands together in agitation.

KiKu shrugged. "This is all I know, but I have been theorizing."

Maura looked at him in anticipation.

"What if the Dinii and Dorak did not leave the chamber of the Mother Bogazkoy of their own volition?" KiKu shifted in his seat and wrapped his cloak closer about him. "You told me that as you struck the death blow to the Black Cacodemon, you could not see what was happening on the other side of the cave."

"That's right," confirmed Maura.

"What if you didn't kill the bastard quickly enough? What if, between the first blow and the deathblow, he had time to utter one last incantation? He was still wearing the amulet you now possess. We do not know of all its powers. What if he willed the Dinii and Dorak away to a magical place, a realm of spirits?"

"KiKu, it would explain so much. It would give an explanation to these horrible dreams I have been having since that terrible day."

"Dreams? You never spoke to anyone about dreams."

Maura smiled a twisted grin. "Do you have spies even in my tent?"

KiKu ignored her question, saying nothing.

Maura took it as a sign he did and congratulated herself on always assuming so. She continued, "I dream of Dorak crying out. I can barely see him except for his eyes, which are wide with fear. He calls to me, pleads for release from what I do not know. I see nothing, but I know he is in a dark and foreboding place." Tears, tinted blue by the gift of the Mother Bogazkoy, fell from her eyes. "I never accepted he was dead." She clutched at her blanket. "I never believed it."

"Then make haste to the temple of Bhuttu. If the Dinii are being seen there even in spirit form, there must exist a portal from which they can return."

"Perhaps this is why they are being seen now. They can make contact, but cannot leave for some reason."

KiKu pointed to the heavy necklace around Maura's neck. "I would expect the amulet you possess is the missing piece. Take the necklace to the temple. If you must, torture the priests until they tell you its secret. Someone there must know something."

Maura looked thoughtful for a moment. "Or you could go."

KiKu shook his head sadly. "My spying days are over. Your balladeers have made my exploits too well known throughout the land," he claimed, not without pride. "I would be discovered."

"A former contact perhaps?" Maura asked, pressing him for a commitment.

"All of the priests know each other well. They would not speak boldly before a stranger."

"How did you find out about the rumors then?"

"I cannot tell you without risking lives, but there are others besides the priests who have witnessed these phantoms."

Maura thought for a moment. "Perhaps we can train someone for a special mission? Someone who is educated and well-versed in literature and religion." She turned to the tiring spylord. "Could you train a person for this mission?"

KiKu rubbed his sleepy eyes. "Yes, but not around here. I would have to take this person to a secluded spot and train him for several months. It could only be done with careful planning."

Extinguishing the small oil lamp, Maura prepared to leave. "You are tired, and I have much to think about."

The prince barely made out the young woman in the dark now. "Great Mother, there is something else I want to tell you."

"What?"

"An old friend awaits you in Bhuttani," he said.

Maura scoffed. "I have no friends in Bhuttani. Of whom do you speak?"

KiKu leaned forward, clasping Maura's mouth with his hand so she would not scream. Softly, he breathed, "Mikkotto!"

6

Maura decided upon a plan.

The army marched forward. The next several weeks were tedious with boredom. Each day, the army journeyed farther and farther from the northern mountains down into the southeastern hill country, finally making its way to the broad band of plains that stretched for almost six hundred miles to Bhuttani, the ultimate goal of the empress. To secure her crown and that of her child, Maura needed to control Bhuttani, the capital and heart of the Bhuttanian Empire. And she needed to capture Jezra, who had fled with the child she had borne Dorak.

Then there were the matters of state. Once Bhuttani was captured, it was not certain whether Hasan Daeg would be assimilated into the Bhuttanian Empire or remain autonomous. It was the hope of most of the

Hasan Daegian nobles that Hasan Daeg would remain independent with only a loosely drawn treaty linking the two nations.

The more conservative elements of Hasan Daegian society wanted to retreat again into isolation, hoping the world would forget them a second time. They wanted nothing to do with the Bhuttanian Empire with its many conflicts and problems. Every day, the Hasan Daegian nobles quietly pursued their goal but were extremely careful in handling the empress.

Assassination was ruled out. No one could get close enough to Maura because the ever-present uultepes stayed steadfast at her side. More than once, a zealot had rushed Maura only to be summarily dispatched by the giant animals' massive claws and lightning fast reflexes. Long-range assassination techniques were abandoned too as having even less chance of success. The empress had been hit many times with poisoned darts. Not only did she survive, but Maura would pull out the darts and, in several minutes, be quickly healed with her aura radiating, shining more brightly than before.

The rays emanating from Maura and her swift heal-ing only roused the Bhuttanians' worship, portraying her to be a demi-goddess. They would leave no stone unturned searching for the assassins.

Then Maura would sit upon the aga's throne, made from the bones of enemies of years gone by, and watch the captured assassins twitch after being hung from the nearest tree. Their boiled white bones would be added to the aga's throne to yellow with age along with the others.

Regardless of the attacks on Maura, the pestilence, the dust and grime, and the uneasy alliance between the Hasan Daegians and the Bhuttanians, the army moved forward. Perhaps at a snail's pace, but still they marched—and wherever the army passed, the country-side began to recover from the terrible toil it had taken under Bhuttanian rule.

The Hasan Daegians immediately began working with farmers and loggers, teaching them new techniques. Sivans were recruited to bring in people who were familiar with the raising and breeding of livestock. Refugees were only too happy to find new homes and work their trades under peaceful conditions. Slowly, the countryside began to recover from the slash and burn policies of Zoar.

Trade was reestablished, and the economy flourished. The Sivans were permitted to barter freely where the empress had established order but were forbidden to trade with those not yet under her control.

The Sivans, believing the Hasan Daegian queen

would reign over most of the caravan routes one day, did nothing to betray her confidence, but privately shook their heads as they passed starving people who remained outside Maura's protection. They felt sick in their hearts when they knew where warehouses full of food were stationed, but dared not betray their loyalty oaths. Helping when they could, they took in many a child from a pleading mother on the roadside. They adopted these children into their clans while Maura looked the other way. Privately, they admitted Maura was made of sterner stuff than her mother, Abisola.

The Sivans were officially apolitical. Their entire culture and economy were based on trade. No other country had been as successful as the Sivans in delivering goods intact and on time. They had become the lifeline for many nations, who depended on them for needed goods and foodstuffs. Sivans were so respected, bandits usually left them alone, but would attack a caravan led by another group traveling right behind them.

When the Hasan Daegians chose isolation and retreated behind their wall of mist created by the caromate plants, it was the Sivans who transported their harvested crops through a corridor specially created for secret trade.

For centuries, the outside world had been using

Hasan Daegian medicinal herbs, hemp ropes, paper, cloth, and food, which they thought originated in a faraway land beyond the water known only to the Sivans who kept the secret. Their discretion was legendary.

Siva was a desert country with borders left unguarded. There was no land to be tilled, timber to be harvested, minerals to be mined, or slaves to be gathered. The few times Siva had been attacked, the Sivans burned everything in sight and committed suicide when captured. While it had not been a happy ending for the hapless victims, it certainly deterred future conquerors from thinking they could find anything of value in Siva.

Throughout the ages, the Sivans had been left alone to do what they did best, which was to distribute the world's wealth and resources through trade.

Like Hasan Daeg, Siva was a matriarchal society. The strange thing was no one outside Siva had ever seen a Sivan woman. Husbands, sons, sons-in-laws, and brothers were sent out into the world to trade while the powers-that-be stayed at home.

The men sported three brands, denoting the clan, the family, and the woman to whom they belonged. Once the brands were seared into the flesh, nothing could revoke those ties except death. There was no divorce in Siva. To ease tension resulting from unhappy marriages, Sivan men took foreign wives in distant lands. No one complained as everyone turned a blind eye and pretended the second wife did not exist. But it was understood by all, the first wife could have the second family eliminated if she so wished.

Happily, most Sivan women were understanding and kind, so all breathed easier under the strict Sivan social codes. Once in a while, a first wife became so enraged that her husband would return to his second home finding it burned to the ground with his family destroyed in the blaze. These men, so filled with grief for their lost families and shamed at having embittered their first wives, committed suicide. It was a rare occurrence but did happen from time to time.

The Sivan men were quiet, industrious, intelligent, and hard negotiators. No written contract was needed with a Sivan. His word was good as gold. It was getting the Sivan to agree in the first place that was usually the sticking point.

It was among a group of Sivans that Timon found the empress. He had asked for his release from service the prior evening, but Rubank refused. To show his displeasure, Timon was late. Now he was worried Rubank would say something to the empress about his pouty behavior.

Maura was on the gigantic platform talking animatedly

with Sivans. She motioned to Timon.

At her side was the ever-silent Rubank, surveying all with his pale gray eyes. Rubank looked up at Timon briefly and continued monitoring the conversation between his blue-skinned ruler and the caramel-skinned Sivans. Timon knew Rubank would need him to translate, as everyone was talking much too fast for the old man to keep up. Rubank, upon taking service with Queen Abisola, had voluntarily cut his tongue out so as not to divulge the queen's secrets. Now that he was older, his hearing was going as well.

Summoning a servant to bring him fresh clay tablets, Timon sighed and hurried over. Kneeling and giving her the Bhuttanian salute, Timon took his place beside Rubank and made mental notes of what was worthy in this conversation to write down. To his surprise, the Sivans were speaking of Bhuttani, having left there many months ago.

Timon studied the Sivans standing before the empress. The men wore beautiful, long-flowing robes of white with finely detailed, embroidered belts and colorful headgear.

Young men wore veils, leaving only their dark, long-lashed eyes exposed. Many a young woman's heart beat faster when she looked into the soulful eyes of a Sivan merchant, but flirt and suggest as she may, nothing would come of it.

One had to be married to a Sivan man to see him let his black hair down the tawny skin of his muscular back and receive kisses from the full, moist lips that graced his face.

But the empress cared not for the beauty of the Sivan men standing before her. Her eyes snapped alive at their mention of Bhuttani. She leaned forward and inhaled every word the Sivans were saying. They were duly upset at the chaos surrounding one of the largest cities in the world and their best markets.

"Great Mother, it is a disgrace. There is no order, even with the White Queen present in the city," complained the elder Sivan, speaking in Anqarian.

"There is only one queen," hissed the High Priestess of Magi, standing behind the empress.

The Sivan merchant paled and bowed very low. Heavy breath expelled from his nose as he lowered his veil. "I express a thousand apologies, Great Mother. I should state Jezra claims to be aganess and her son the rightful heir to the aga's throne. I only repeat what she has stated."

Maura waved his apology aside. She knew her claim to the aga's throne hung tenuously in the balance.

Jezra had as much legal right to claim the Bhuttanian Empire for her son by Dorak as Maura did for Dorak's daughter. Maura was determined to beat Jezra at all costs. She just had to be cunning and keep those Bhuttanians, who remained at her side, loyal to her cause. All in all, Maura believed it was going to be fate that determined if she entered Bhuttani as aganess or found her head on a chopping block. Maura would do anything to ensure her daughter's future, and gaining absolute power was the only means to prevent her daughter from being hunted down and killed by Jezra.

Maura asked, "Why do you call Jezra the White Queen?"

"The Buttanians refer to her as the White Queen because of her golden hair and fair complexion, and you are the Blue Queen due to your blue flesh. The common people use these terms for it is easier for them to remember rather than formal titles. No disrespect is intended by either name."

"None taken. Go on," instructed Maura impatiently.

The Sivan looked cautiously at the empress before continuing. "The city is divided into three parts with Jezra controlling the largest area. She has power over the palace, the oldest sections of the city, the west gate, and the temple of Bhuttu. Cappet, a petty thug, controls much of the eastern part of the city. His part includes the river docks. He has access to food and oil."

"Wait!" cried Maura, holding up her hand. "What of

the temple? Is the temple building intact? What of the priests?"

The eyes of the Sivan merchant revealed surprise. "Great Mother, I was not aware you had become a follower of Bhuttu."

Maura flinched. How stupid of her to show interest in the temple. There could be spies listening to this conversation. She had to be more patient. "I worry for the sake of my people, half of whom are Bhuttanian now. They revere their god, Bhuttu."

The elder Sivan merchant breathed easier. He disapproved of the harsh and cruel faith of Bhuttu and would not have liked to report to his superiors he suspected the new empress might be a follower of the ancient dark religion. "The temple has suffered very little damage, but the priests have been conducting strange purification rites for many months. There are rumors the temple is possessed."

"Tell me more about this Cappet."

"He is an opportunist. He saw a gap in Jezra's control and took advantage of it. I hate to say this, but he seems to be an able administrator. Of the three sectors, his people are the best fed and suffer the least."

"And the third section?"

"Controlled by a venerated general of Zoar's, a man named Prosperot. He controls little that is important and is in a weak position, but he is respected by all and is left alone."

"I know him. He was one of Zoar's main generals, along with Alexanee. He fled after Aga Dorak went missing. What does he control?"

"He guards the bones of Zoar and his ancestors."

Maura started to laugh. "A graveyard. He protects dead men." She paused for a moment. "The Bhuttanians do not bury their dead. They burn the bodies and scatter the ashes."

The Sivan merchant looked about him sheepishly. "Great Mother, the Bhuttanians are very involved with ancestor worship where their nobles are concerned. Bones of high-ranking persons left from the funeral pyre are taken back to one specific location where they are interred into the special crypts. That Prosperot would take this assignment without being ordered speaks very highly of his esteemed character."

Pulling a strand of blowing hair away from her face, the High Priestess said, "I thought Zoar was cremated in Camaroon outside the Hasan Daegian border. The empress saw him being burned."

"Oh no, Wise One, his bones were taken back immediately after the ceremonial fire," replied the elder Sivan merchant, who stealthily nudged his companion. He had thought the Magi scholars were all-knowing.

This mistake of the High Priestess would prove to be valuable information to the Sivans in the future.

The empress took in the subtle nudge of the Sivan merchant to his companion and wished the High Priestess would keep her mouth closed. She, herself, had already made a costly blunder during this interview, and now the High Priestess had made another. "I wish to speak with the Sivans in private," she said abruptly.

Timon wanted to kick the High Priestess, who now looked very contrite as she climbed down off the platform. The conversation was becoming interesting, and now he would not be privy to it. He waited until the very last second before the guards pushed him toward the stairs. Blast it! For once, he genuinely wanted to be involved with the empress and was losing his chance. He thought of shouting the suggestion that he remain and take notes but caught the empress' icy glare. He hurried along with Rubank and the other advisors. Pushed away from the rolling platform for at least ten feet, Timon could hear nothing.

The empress had leaned very close to the Sivans and used a fan to cover her mouth. Now no one would be able to read her lips.

Squinting against the late summer sun, Timon saw the Bhuttanian cavalry approaching. He scampered out of the way of the great warhorses only to be scolded by a sullen cook, who was trying to navigate his wagon out of the way as well. Whirlwinds of dust were stirred up by the massive hooves of the giant steeds.

Timon, choking, called to a water boy. Holding up the leather bag, Timon took a long draught of the water, not letting the bag touch his lips, as was the custom. The water was clear so it must have been purified by Hasan Daegians. They refused to drink cloudy water.

Making his way back, Timon found the empress gone from the platform. He looked frantically about him. Grabbing a soldier trudging next to him, Timon asked, "Have you seen the empress?"

The foot soldier, weary from many miles of marching, pointed his lance at the western horizon. "I saw that dark head of hers go over there. She was walking with two Sivans."

"Thanks, my good man," said Timon, flipping the soldier a copper coin.

The soldier caught the coin in mid-air. "Anytime," he replied, waving a chipper goodbye.

Timon trotted through a column of marching soldiers, ignoring officers cursing him for causing their soldiers to falter. The hurrying scribe called out his apologies, only to be met by fierce growls from a commander getting his men into marching rhythm again.

While dodging soldiers, he came upon Hasan Daegian scouts returning to give their reports.

Astride their small ponies, the Hasan Daegian riders looked ridiculous next to any Bhuttanian mount, which was almost three times the size. But the Hasan Daegian ponies were gaining respect among the Bhuttanians for their hardiness and the way they could maneuver during a battle.

Timon waved to some of the Hasan Daegian riders he knew and darted in between the horses.

A mangy murex caught sight of Timon and ran after him, trying to bite his ankles. A small girl ran up to the murex and, after spanking him for being naughty, put the chastised animal on a rope and led him away.

"Serves him right," muttered Timon.

Through a haze of wagons filled with wives, children, and servants belonging to various Bhuttanian officers, Timon could see the empress walking with the Sivan merchants. Timon strained his neck, searching the crowd around her.

Rubank and the High Priestess did not follow at a discreet distance. In fact, he didn't see them anywhere. Only the Imperial guards were present, and they were busy keeping pesky animals and curious children from bothering the empress.

The uultepes were lying down on a small mound,

eyeing the women and children who were watching them. One of the uultepes yawned and rolled on its back, stirring up dust. It sneezed and rubbed its face with its paw.

Timon walked carefully around them at a great distance. He had never seen them attack anyone without cause, but it never hurt to be careful.

Suddenly, a company of thirty Hasan Daegian horsewomen with two riderless ponies rode up to the empress.

The uultepes were immediately by her side.

The horses, smelling the great beasts, whinnied and pawed the ground nervously. Their riders had a hard time controlling them.

Timon saw the empress give something to one of the Sivan merchants. The merchant took the object and tucked it in his robe. Both merchants bowed and allowed themselves to be helped in mounting the small Hasan Daegian ponies.

The Sivans, being natural riders, had no problem controlling the skittish horses. They waved goodbye to the empress, turning their ponies to the west. The rest of the riders surrounded the merchants and galloped away at high speed.

Timon's curiosity was piqued. The tall scribe approached the empress, coming to rest six feet from her.

"May I approach the empress?"

Maura turned. Her face seemed strained but, at the sight of the young scribe, relaxed. "Yes, Timon, you may come closer."

"Does the Great Mother need anything?"

The empress thought for a moment and smiled. "I don't know what you mean, Master Timon."

Timon shifted his weight. "Do you need me to record your meeting with the Sivans?"

Maura laughed out loud. "Oh, Timon, you should be more subtle if you wish to discover something."

Feeling the blood rush to his face, Timon could not help but return her smile. Maura's laugh was infectious.

"How old are you, Timon ben Ibin Moab?"

"Seventeen, Your Majesty."

"You are not much younger than I." Maura cocked her head to one side as if to better study the youth. "Do I seem very old to you?"

"Well," Timon paused, not knowing what he should say. Her face was unlined but seemed old much like his mother's.

"Tell the truth, young scribe. How old do you think I am? Really."

"My age, Great Mother."

"Timon, you are terrible at flattery. The truth is I'll be twenty-three at the next full moon. The war started on my eighteenth birthday." Maura's smiled drifted away. "I would wager you still feel young. I would give almost anything to feel that way again. Enjoy your youth and innocence, Timon, while you can, because in one heartbeat, something could happen to make you feel old and corrupt."

Maura held up a finger. "Just one heartbeat."

7

The army marched.

Scouts from Jezra's rebels could be seen in the distance, taking progress reports on the moving city that was the enemy army. Maura never had them pursued, letting the wary spies watch as if to say they were too unimportant for her to be concerned about.

Across the steppes, the army traveled at a leisurely pace from one paltry waterhole to the next. Maura was disgusted with the water on the plains. It was brown and dirty with a strong sulfur odor—not like the clean, pure water at home that glistened under the warming sun. Her countrywomen were alike in their abhorrence of the natural conditions outside their homeland. Any water the Hasan Daegians or their animals consumed had to be strained and purified with herbs. Hasan Daegian physicians warned the Bhuttanians not to drink the water without purification, but the Bhuttanians would laugh good-naturedly and then come down with a case of dysentery.

Fleas and lice were other problems repelling the tidy Hasan Daegians. They were forever rubbing ointments and lotions on their skin, trying to preserve some semblance of grooming while ridding themselves of parasites living on their bodies.

The Bhuttanians shaved the hair from their bodies, following the practice of the Hasan Daegians, and rubbed zelkova juice everywhere. While the juice had little effect on lice, it did repel the biting flies and good company as well.

Timon succumbed to the prevalent practices and shaved his entire body, except for his head. While he would wear the potent Bhuttanian juice to repel crawly things from his warm-colored skin, he also tried some of the Hasan Daegian lotions, which at the moment were not working. He slapped the side of his neck and, catching some gnats, squeezed them between his fingers. He wanted desperately to reach under his tunic and scratch his unmentionables but didn't dare. Timon had caught the empress scrutinizing him now and then, and he certainly did not want to be found scratching his backside or worse when she glanced his way.

The tall, lanky scribe wondered why the empress

should show any curiosity in him whatsoever. Her interest in him had grown with the arrival of KiKu. He wondered if it had anything to do with the growing tension between the empress and KiKu. The prince of Hittal could no longer hide his dismay with the empress for never publicly asking him to dine with her or to be in her general company. It would be a great slight for any royal person, and the fact the Bhuttanians now openly laughed at him caused the wound to cut deeper. Though KiKu's tent was still next to Maura's, most people regarded this as the empress protecting KiKu from his many enemies while in her care and nothing more.

KiKu became less guarded with his emotions and could be seen scowling at the empress, which was immediately reported to her.

Maura merely tossed her head and snorted, but Timon knew that these incidents would cause further estrangement between the former allies.

When the empress organized a celebratory dinner for her birthday and did not ask KiKu to join, it was more than the Hittal prince could endure. He packed up his goods, his wives, and servants, leaving the camp in a huff one morning.

There was talk among the Bhuttanians they should go after him, as KiKu did not ask royal permission to leave the encampment. But the empress said she was glad to be rid of him, and they should not waste their valuable time on a petty, deposed potentate. Within hours of his departure, KiKu was forgotten and life went on as before. Only Timon seemed to ponder the strange relationship between KiKu and the empress.

The empress studied local maps as before, questioned Timon endlessly about his life and his homeland as before, took loveless lovers as before, fed the uultepes from her plate as before. She seemed relatively unconcerned about KiKu's hurt feelings.

Timon shuddered at the thought of KiKu. He would not like having the spylord angry with him.

KiKu was said to have a hundred disguises, which he could assume and move about anywhere undetected. He could be the washerman who cleaned one's shirts. He could be the servant who filled one's goblet. He could be a Sivan merchant trading rare cloth. He could be the soldier standing guard at the door. He could be the woman who enticed unsuspecting men into "her" tent.

And he had a hundred ways to kill his victims. The shirt could have a poisoned needle in the cuff. The goblet could be laced with a potent drug. The rare cloth could suffocate without notice. The soldier could kill with a single blow from his sword and melt into the confused crowd. The "woman" could use her hands to snap a customer's neck as he removed his clothing.

Timon dug into his pockets, rummaging for a writing stick while he considered KiKu's potential for danger. No, he would not like the spylord to be angry with him for any reason.

The empress, concerned the animals needed a well-deserved rest, stopped near the original tribal border of Bhuttan before its expansion into an empire.

Her Bhuttani soldiers were anxious to see their families again, but waited patiently with characteristic Bhuttanian sentiment—a great deal of cursing and complaining. They realized exhausted horses were no good to them in the battle that was surely coming.

The Hasan Daegians were content to use the time to bathe, rinse their hair, and wash their clothes. Their servants ignored the snide comments of the Bhuttanians as they hauled water from a nearby river. "At least we don't smell like a whore's backside," the Hasan Daegians sniped.

This comment would only make the Bhuttanians roar with laughter. "I'd like to have the money a good whore would have," a foot soldier yelled back, "and if that meant that I have the stink of twelve men on me— so be it."

"That's what you Hasan Daegian women need—a

good Bhuttanian man to cover you like a stallion covers a mare," cried out another Bhuttanian.

A Hasan Daegian servant, who was drying his lady's hair in front of her tent, bellowed, "Our women don't need dirty Bhuttanians when they have refined, cultured men to marry."

The Bhuttanians hooted and hurled clods of dirt at the Hasan Daegian's tent. "Who said anything about marrying? We just want a quick poke and then be on our way."

The Hasan Daegian woman, who was having her hair dried, threw the towel off her head in disgust. She stood with her arms akimbo. "Quick, indeed. I'm sure it would be as Bhuttanian men cannot 'hold' for very long just as they cannot hold their liquor." She held up her pinky finger and wiggled it. "Of course, I hear there is not much to work with."

A Bhuttanian stood up from his fire and began raising his tunic. "I'll show you what a real man looks like, not those runty lap dogs you pillow with."

The Hasan Daegian woman pulled her sword from its scabbard hanging from her chair. "Hold it there, soldier, or I'll have you for dinner in more ways than one."

Other Bhuttanian soldiers, watching the exchange, burst into laughter and threw more clods at Hasan

Daegian women now gathering in force. Brandishing a sword or dagger, the women began advancing on the mouthy Bhuttanian soldiers.

The Bhuttanian men, seeing their Hasan Daegian comrades were serious, stopped bantering. "They can never take a joke," complained one soldier. "They are always so damned serious."

"Our honor is not a subject for your entertainment," retorted one Hasan Daegian woman, dressed in her archer's uniform. "Apologize for your insulting remarks to my countrywoman or draw your weapons."

"I would rather stick my head in a bucket of borax shit," sneered the Bhuttanian, pulling his tunic down. His hand rested near his dagger's hilt. He moved in an aggressive swagger toward the knot of Hasan Daegian women.

"Halt, you stupid swine!" roared a Bhuttanian officer, who was hurrying toward his tent to change into ceremonial armor. "The royal consul is approaching. Be sharp about your manners."

Immediately, those present hid their weapons and scanned their surroundings for Rubank, worried that word of their argument had already made its way back to the empress. All knew they could lose their heads for wrangling in public. The empress kept a tight rein on any quarreling amongst her soldiers, especially now they were entering Bhuttan proper. The Bhuttanians quickly scattered while the Hasan Daegian women stood at attention, waiting for the worst.

A small pocket of dignitaries, dressed in the blue robes of the Hasan Daegian court, made its way toward the small knot of women. Next to an impressive older man walked a youth dressed in the brown robe of a scribe. He was speaking to the older man. The Hasan Daegian women bowed low as they recognized the Royal Consul Rubank and the Royal Scribe Timon.

Rubank stopped in front of the Hasan Daegian warriors and peered into the sky. He placed his hand over his eyes and scanned the horizon. He wrote on a wet tablet given to him by Timon, who translated every word loudly so all could listen easily—even those hiding in their tents.

Timon addressed the other officials standing with them. "My Lord Rubank says he is baffled. He thought only a moment ago he heard the distant rumbling of an unfortunate storm, but now the sky is perfectly clear without any angry countenance. He asks his learned friends to account for this."

The other officials tried to appear very serious and not smile at the sight of the Hasan Daegian women straining their necks to listen.

One elderly man spoke, "I would venture, my Lord

Consul, that an unexpected calm front came into the area, breaking up the current tumultuous weather pattern."

The officials glanced out of the corners of their eyes and saw frightened Bhuttanians peeking from their tents, after having sent their slaves out to work so they might better hear and report back.

The consul wrote again.

Timon read out loud, "My Lord Consul wishes to express calm weather will be expected for the duration of our march." Timon watched Rubank mark his reed in the wet clay. "And he thinks anything else would not be tolerated by the empress, not even the most innocent of breezes."

Rubank resumed his walk down the lane flanked by rows of tents. The other officials followed suit.

Timon turned his head toward the Hasan Daegian women and winked. He hurried his steps to catch up with Rubank.

The Hasan Daegian women relaxed their stance and breathed easier.

Rubank glanced back and shot them an icy stare.

The women gasped and rushed into their tents, not appearing again until nightfall when they shared food with their Bhuttanian brethren as a friendly gesture.

The Bhuttanian men were not keen on the feast,

which consisted mainly of vegetables. They liked meat, but they ate the dishes nonetheless, and many found them not unpleasant. They, in turn, gave the Hasan Daegians small tokens that they would give to their wives or mistresses, not knowing what else to give a woman.

The warrior women looked down upon their gifts of small coins or scented handkerchiefs in disbelief. These were not proper gifts for comrades in war. They would rather have had sandal laces or a grinding stone to keep their weapons sharp, but wishing to keep the peace, they graciously thanked the Bhuttanian men.

The Bhuttanians sheepishly stared at the ground, wishing to be anywhere but with the large and imposing Hasan Daegian women. They were glad their females were petite —easier to control. Still, they stole glances at the Hasan Daegian women's full hips and breasts, wondering.

Timon, finished with his official duties for Rubank, strolled through the camp again. He studied the hide-covered tents of the Bhuttanians, which dulled next to the brightly colored cloth pavilions of the Hasan Daegians. He pondered how the Hasan Daegians kept themselves from getting wet during a heavy rain, but the tents were always dry on the inside no matter the weather. In fact, Hasan Daegians usually looked very healthy, and it was a known fact most of them kept all of their teeth until their deaths. Timon thought that was amazing. He put his finger in his mouth and felt the gaps between his back teeth. He wished he had beautiful teeth like the Hasan Daegians, but at least his were not rotting like most of the older Bhuttanian men. *Bad diet*, thought Timon.

As he passed, many people, both high and lowborn, nodded or hailed him. Most people knew of the young Bhuttanian from the outer steppes of the empire who translated the thoughts of Rubank, consul for the empress. Some believed Timon might be an important man one day and went out of their way to make themselves known to him. Timon, being without guile, thought they were being friendly and responded in kind. He didn't realize he was being sought out and cultivated on purpose.

A young courier trotted on a well-worn path, perusing the throng of soldiers, cobblers, cooks, slaves, and animals mingling back and forth. Spying Timon talking with a young Hasan Daegian woman, he scampered over to Timon and pulled on the scribe's long sleeve. Timon pushed the young boy away, continuing to flirt with the young Hasan Daegian archer.

"Master, Master, you must come! The empress has summoned you!" breathlessly exclaimed the boy.

"What?" asked Timon, incredulously.

"You must hurry," repeated the young boy. "She wants you to come quickly."

Timon swallowed hard and bid the Hasan Daegian archer a hasty goodbye.

She waved sympathetically.

No one wanted to be summoned by the empress. Maura was predictable only in that her moods ranged from a simmering quiet to a raging tempest. She was not known for her good temper. A sullen, withdrawn woman at most times, she lacked the grace of her cunning but ruthless husband Dorak.

Even Dorak's enemies thought he had possessed a certain charm, which seemed to make his evil less—evil.

While the empress was certainly more honorable than her former husband, she was not much of a wit or biting satirist—behaviors which made court life bearable for most Bhuttanians. A capable but boring monarch was a burden no one wanted to share, least of all Timon, as he hurried toward the royal tent. What could she want of him?

Stumbling through the entrance of the royal pavilion, he was waved back into Maura's private room by the chamber attendant. Straightening his tunic and smoothing down his hair, he asked the guards to announce him. He was told to wait as the empress was bathing her daughter. A chair was brought for Timon, and as he waited, he cleaned the dirt encased between his toes. A servant, bringing a clean cloth, chided Timon for not changing his sandals.

"I didn't have time," hissed Timon. "Hold your tongue, or I'll make you eat this mud!" he snapped at the woman.

The servant sniffed the air as though a foul stench had been emitted and turned her heels on Timon.

"Servants," muttered Timon, exasperated.

One of the lads-in-waiting came out and bade Timon to enter. "She's in a good mood," he whispered close to Timon's ear. "You are fortunate."

Timon nodded his thanks and entered.

Maura was sitting on her bed in a loosely tied robe playing with Princess Dyanna.

As she bent over her daughter, Timon could see her breasts sway. They were full and firm. Embarrassed, Timon inspected his clean feet.

Maura ignored the presence of Timon as she tickled her daughter's tiny feet and pulled the squirming princess away from the edge of the bed. The baby started to pout until the empress blew on her fat belly, causing the princess to squeal with delight. The happy mother hugged her daughter and then handed her over to a nurse.

When Maura turned to Timon, there were no remnants of the happy, contented mother he had witnessed just seconds before. Maura showed her calculating, mistrustful expression always given to the public. The sudden change in Maura's countenance chilled Timon.

The empress stretched out on the bed like one of her uultepes lounging on the floor. "Timon, I am bored. I wish to go out on a hunt tomorrow. Since you claim to know this area, you will act as my guide."

"What shall be the object of your hunt, Great Mother?"

"I want to kill something big, something we can eat later that day; something the minstrels will sing about."

"Then for game that big, we shall have to go toward the foothills. It will take more than a day to reach our destination."

"Won't that take us deep into Jezra's territory?"

"Not if we go due north. As long as we don't turn east, we shall be all right, if Your Majesty's scouts are correct in their assessment of Jezra's movements."

Maura cast him a sidelong glance. "To suggest my scouts might be wrong would be to suggest I might be wrong." She turned away from him. "Even when I'm wrong, I am right."

"I understand your meaning, Great Mother."

"To understand my meaning is good for the only

son of a poor widow from an obscure village in the middle of nowhere."

"Great Mother, I am no one."

"It still seems strange to me that you were selected by Zoar out of thousands of boys placed in his service."

"I am grateful to the gods."

"I thought you believed in only one god."

"I was speaking figuratively. Perhaps I should say I was born under a lucky star."

"It would seem you were, Timon. A very lucky star." Maura paused and tightened her robe about her. "Come here. I want a better look at you."

Timon ventured closer.

"Closer. The light is dim." Timon moved toward the empress silently, hoping the uultepes would not attack him. One of them growled in a subdued manner.

The empress bade Timon to stop. She studied him as though trying to discover a secret. The way she leered at him made Timon feel naked.

"Have you a woman?"

Timon stood at attention—his heart pounding in his ears. Timon blushed to the very roots of his hair. He wanted to say yes—many women, but she would know he was lying. "No, Great Mother, I have never known the pleasure of a woman's bed."

"Or a boy's?"

"No, Great Mother."

"Are you an ascetic?"

"My mother made me swear an oath of purity until I was married."

Maura reached up and stroked Timon's black hair. She leaned over and took a deep smell of him. "Why would your mother make you take such an oath?" She tenderly kissed his earlobe.

"My mother was concerned there not be any paternity entanglements." The empress' hot breath on his skin made Timon both angry and woozy with desire. He wanted to be gone from this temptress.

"Why would a peasant woman care about such a matter? Only nobles worry about such things." Maura slowly rubbed Timon's chest.

"My mother is a chaste and virtuous woman, even though a peasant," spat out Timon, his upper body heaving heavily. He gave the empress a look of disdain.

"I see I have insulted you, Timon. It was not my intention, I assure you."

"Your Majesty has not insulted me. As you have so said, even when you are wrong, you are right."

Maura clasped her hands to her heart and feigned a blow to the chest. "You have injured me with my own words. Serves me right. Keep your virtue for now, Timon. There is no way I want to go against a righteous mother. I will catch up with you after a Hasan Daegian maiden has tumbled you." She picked up a goblet and took a drink of colla water. "You may go. I will see you at dawn."

Timon bowed low and retreated from Maura's presence. Once outside her chambers, he ran to his own tent.

Upon hearing Timon's hasty footfalls, Maura chuckled to herself.

From a darkened corner of Maura's room appeared the High Priestess of Magi. She gathered her bluish-green robes, waiting for the empress to address her.

Maura looked at her with bright eyes. "I don't know whether to congratulate his mother for his chastity or be insulted at his scorn."

"I think he is a most congenial choice, Great Mother."

"I pray to Mekonia he is the right one."

"I am sure you have made the correct selection."

"He'd better be, or I shall ride into Bhuttani without backup."

"I know this is a painful topic, but perhaps you should accept Dorak might be dead."

Maura threw the goblet against the wall of her chamber. "NEVER!"

The High Priestess bowed her head. "I have caused

my sovereign grief. May I be excused, Great Mother?"

"Get out." Maura sank into a chair. She moaned in despair, her features contorting in misery. "Dorak," she whispered to drifting currents of air. "If you hear me, have faith. I will come, never fear. I will come. I will come for you."

8

The Great Divigi winced in pain.

He tried to spread his wings but was met with resistance from his companion.

"Get those damn feathers out of my face. I can't breathe," Dorak muttered.

"So sorry," mumbled Iegani, the Great Divigi, "but if we don't move them every so often, we get severe cramps in our shoulders. They are heavy, you know," he said, referring to his massive wings.

"And useless to us here."

"I agree my wings have been of little use since we arrived, but who knows about the future?"

"If we have a future."

"That's pitiful to hear from the Great Aga, Master of the World. One would think you would exude a little more confidence."

"The devil take thee, Iegani."

Iegani raised an eyebrow. "How Anqarian of you, Dorak."

Dorak chortled. "The influence of my first wife, I'm afraid."

"Ah, yes, Jezra. For such a moral and brave people, I would bet you were a little disappointed in Jezra's behavior after she arrived at court."

"That's an understatement. It was thought an Anqarian bride would be a positive influence. Little did we know," Dorak said before breaking off.

"Jezra would take an interest in the black arts," filled in Iegani. "You can hardly blame her for indulging. After all, you were dipping into the pot so to speak."

"I hardly thought my wife would team up with my wizard and try to usurp my throne."

"Oh, you thought she would be on your side," retorted Iegani, "especially after Zoar burned her city and killed her father. Of course, she welcomed you with open arms on your wedding night."

"Her father committed suicide," replied Dorak with grim brevity.

"That makes all the difference."

Dorak spat, "Are we going to quarrel again? After all, your hands are not without blood on them. Weren't there rumors you murdered your lover?"

"I did not want to. She left me no recourse."

"Oh, well, that makes all the difference."

"Shut up, you puny little man. You know nothing. You are nothing but a blight upon the world." Iegani's eyes flashed like molten gold.

Dorak's anger swelled like a tight ball in his stomach. He curled his fist and struck Iegani under the chin.

Iegani's extended his hand, and a razor-sharp talon was released from under his skin. He moved in for the kill.

"STOP THIS!" Gitar, Empress of the Dinii, stood several feet from the dueling Dini and the aga. "I GAVE YOU BOTH A COMMAND!" Her voice boomed and reverberated off the walls of their prison.

Reluctantly, Iegani retracted his long nail. He glared at Dorak.

"I understand you two argue to take your minds off our problems, but it is wasted energy. One of these days, you will both go too far, and then where shall we be?"

Dorak nodded in agreement and bowed very low. "My Lady, you are correct as usual. The pain we cause each other takes our minds off our greater anguish."

"And guilt?"

"Yes, Empress Gitar, but my guilt is my burden that I do not wish to inflict upon you," responded Dorak.

"Then do not do so, Lord Dorak. I have enough to contemplate," said Gitar. She turned toward Iegani. "Have you been able to establish contact with Maura?"

Iegani shook his head. "She just has vague impressions. At present, Maura is acting on gut instinct. As long as she thinks Dorak might be alive, she will search for us. You must stay alive, Great Aga. If she thinks there is a chance for your survival, Maura will stop at nothing to find you."

Dorak closed his eyes, thinking of sweet memories with Maura. "That you must go into the fires of hell to find me, be it so, Maura."

Exchanging glances with Gitar, Iegani said, "See, I told you he was turning into an Anqarian."

"Just keep him alive, Iegani. It is your meddling that got us into this situation in the first place."

Iegani winced at the words of his niece.

Gitar watched a priest burn incense upon the eternal flame to Bhuttu. She reached out to touch his arm, but her hand went through his flesh. "How strange. We stand beside them watching their every movement, but they can neither hear nor see us," remarked Gitar.

The priest looked up, feeling an unexplained draft. He shivered and tightened his shawl around his shoulders.

Dorak took out his dagger and stabbed the priest in

the chest.

Feeling a sharp twinge near his heart, the priest murmured an incantation before running away. Dorak swung around laughing. Seeing the stark eyes of Gitar, he stopped short.

"We are even less than the wisps of ghosts," complained a forlorn Gitar. She sat glumly on the steps leading up to Bhuttu's bronze statue.

Dorak went over to her. "My Lady, we are not without hope. Maura will come for us. I know it. And Iegani says she continues to wear the amulet."

"But will she make the connection? We never taught her about magic. We didn't believe in it. The Dinii know nothing about such arts."

The aga patted her on the arm. "She's a quick study."

Sitting on the marble floor and leaning against a massive column, the weary Dini empress looked as small as a child.

Dorak felt a stab of pity that a creature so noble as she should be reduced thus. He leaned over to comfort the empress when Iegani grabbed his arm.

"Did you hear that? Shhhh."

Dorak and Iegani peered into the darkened recess of the temple sanctuary. They had learned only the area in which they stood was illuminated. The rest of their prison remained dark and forbidding. Creatures, other than themselves, were caught up in their world and not all of them were friendly.

"What is it?" asked Dorak, unsheathing his dagger.

A slithering sound emanated from one corner, and Iegani saw something move behind the massive statue of Bhuttu. "There!" he said, pointing.

Dorak squinted his eyes. While the base of the statue was clear, the top portion was cloudy and out of focus until it receded into a thick grey mist. Dorak pulled Gitar to her feet. "Lady, I think it is time we should rejoin the others. There is safety in numbers."

Gitar, towered over Dorak, confused. "I am so tired, Dorak. Won't you let me sleep?"

Iegani pulled on one of her wings. "As they say, there is no rest for the wicked."

The regal Dini snarled. "I am not wicked. You are not suggesting that, are you, Iegani?"

"No, my niece, it is a figure of speech. We both know that of the two of us, I am the evil one."

"I would say evil is too harsh a word. Well-intentioned gone mad is more correct."

"You are very kind, Empress."

Gitar gave a lop-sided grin. "Of course, we both know the real evil here is Dorak."

Dorak bowed very low to them both. "You mark me

well, Lady. That you would have me in your presence reflects your tolerance and graciousness."

Narrowing her eyes, Gitar took a sharp finger and poked Dorak in the chest, "Little man, I do believe your words carry more than one meaning."

Iegani sneered, "This is the most fun I have had in days, but something behind the statue sounds very big, and I am a coward in my old age. I wish to leave now and join the others."

Dorak turned to Gitar. "I think he is being sarcastic."

Iegani reattached their ropes of woven feathers to each other's waists, so they would not become separated in the darkness into which they would have to flee. He had not quite finished when a slimy green-scaled creature with great black lines on its back emerged from behind the statue into the open sanctuary.

Iegani caught only a glance of a moving green streak while wrapping the rope around his wrist. He pushed Gitar into the darkness. "Run," he cried, "and don't look back!"

Gitar and Dorak did not need to be told twice. They ran into the dark where they would be able to hide from whatever was hunting them, or, at least, they hoped. Each felt a tug on the other end where the rest of the outcast Dinii awaited for them.

As he ran, Dorak yanked back a signal code. The rope was being quickly reeled in, helping to guide the great aga and his bird-like companions. Because of their large size, Gitar and Iegani were more cautious in their escape than the quick and agile Dorak. They were in a building not designed to accommodate the legendary Dinii and their massive wingspan. Doorways were not wide enough, the floors were too slippery for their taloned feet, and the ceilings were too low. Though they could pass through stone and wood in their present form, they had great difficulty doing so. It gave them headaches.

Gitar looked back to gauge their escape. She spied the snake-like creature behind them.

It reared up and opened its gaping mouth, exposing hundreds of razor-sharp teeth. Gitar had never seen a creature so hideous in form and gasped in outright fear at its horrible appearance. She had never known fear such as this, not even that ghastly night when Dorak's minions swept into City of the Peaks, destroying her home forever.

Stumbling, Gitar could not regain her balance and fell on the cold marble floor. She cried out as the creature loomed over her. Empress Gitar, long astute in the ways of killing, and now fearing she was about to be devoured herself, instinctively exposed her talons and bared her teeth. If she were going to die, she would try to take the hideous creature with her, thus saving her friends. "Prepare to die!" she hissed at the drooling and loathing viper.

The serpent lowered its head as a foul stench emanated from its mouth.

Gitar spat at it and cursed its birth. Swinging her powerful arms at the snapping serpent, she raked her razor-sharp talons across the bridge of its nose. The creature seemed startled and sensing its hesitation, Gitar swung again, digging in deeper. Glancing out of the corner of her eye, she saw Dorak rush the creature and plunge his dagger into the viper's fetid skin while Iegani stood on the other side of the creature thrusting with his talons.

Purple syrupy liquid gushed forth from the creature as it rose higher, howling in pain.

A flash of light exploded, blinding Gitar and the others. Dorak covered his eyes with his left arm but kept stabbing until he felt the flesh of the creature no more. Confused, he lowered his arm and blinked heavily. He heard Iegani stumble to Gitar and ask her if she was all right.

Helping the empress to her feet, Iegani felt the last of his strength taxed. He wished desperately to sit down somewhere. Confident his niece had not been injured, he turned toward Dorak only to find the aga trembling, his dagger hanging limply at his side. Iegani followed Dorak's gaze and gasped.

On a shimmering, gaseous cloud, hovering off the floor, stood a spectral vision of Zoar, Dorak's father!

For a few seconds, Iegani stood stunned until he managed to find his voice. "Why aren't you dead?"

A small chuckle issued from the transparent form of the former aga. "Perhaps I am dead, and you are dead with me."

Iegani pondered this for a moment. "I don't think so," he said, although he was not sure.

"My father is dead. YOU ARE NOT ZOAR!" cried out Dorak.

"You betrayed me, son! Do you not feel the evil of your deed has undone our people?" snorted Zoar, fixing his withering gaze upon Dorak.

"I KILLED THEE!" shouted Dorak. "IT CAN-NOT BE!" Dorak trembled with fear and loathing.

Both Iegani and Gitar looked askance at Dorak. Iegani stepped beside Dorak, placing his hand on Dorak's shoulder. "The apparition is not he. Do not fear this bloated shadow of corruption. We cannot speak with the dead, my son."

Instantly, the milky semblance of Zoar disappeared, and a new form took its place.

"Zedek!" cried out Dorak, oddly relieved at the wizard's countenance.

"I always did like to make a grand entrance," announced the Black Cacodemon, irritated his disguise was seen through so quickly. "Did I give you a fright, Dorak?"

"What do you want with us?" asked Gitar, pushing Iegani aside. "Where are we?"

The Black Cacodemon's thin lips broke into a smile. "You are where I have put you."

"And where is that?" repeated Gitar, breathing heavily. That she was under the control of such an odious man made Gitar furious. As she talked, spittle flew out of her mouth.

"My dear Empress, there is no use getting yourself worked up into a lather. No one would be here at all if Maura had not stabbed me in the heart and stolen my amulet." The wizard waved a hand slightly, and his cloud floated closer to them. "I had only a few seconds to mumble an incantation, but without the amulet, one can only do so much," he said, shrugging. "I could only get this far, which was fortunate."

"Why is that?" asked Dorak, barely being able to hide his contempt for his former ally.

"I was trying to send you all to the bowels of hell," he smiled viciously. "Yes, the Anqarians are right about hell, but I digress. We were all thrown in together." He looked about him. "Otherwise, I would like it here. I was in need of a rest anyway, and this would have been the perfect hiding place to recuperate until I could re-emerge. Of course, life is not without its problems. All of you followed. Or I followed you. Now the mere presence of so many beings in the in-between-world disturbs the harmony." The wizard peered closer at Gitar. "The vibrations are not what they should be."

"I am so sorry," Gitar replied sarcastically.

"Ah, well."

"You have not answered me. Where are we?" asked Dorak impatiently.

The wizard winced, "Dorak, I never thought you were very perceptive. It should be obvious where we are." The wizard stared at Iegani. "I would wager that you know."

Gitar and Dorak looked at Iegani. The owl-like man sighed heavily. "Apparently, in a state of flux."

"Speak clearly, man," barked Dorak.

"Dorak, you said this place was the temple of Bhuttu. An actual place with people coming and going who we can see and hear, but not touch or contact. They can neither see, hear, nor touch us as well. They do not know we exist." Iegani held out his hands helplessly. "We are neither dead nor alive, but somehow we exist in the spirit world. We are in the Nether Realm."

The Black Cacodemon snapped his fingers. "Correct," he hollered. "It has only taken you years to figure that out."

"Years?" gasped Gitar. "We have only been here for a few hours."

Howling with laughter, the Black Cacodemon grabbed at his stomach. "Oh, dear Lady, you have been here for two years—almost three." He laughed again. "This is so rich."

Dorak advanced upon the wizard's cloud with his dagger pitched forward. "Do not laugh at her confusion. You are not even fit to speak to her."

The wizard feigned surprise. "You are defending the honor of the Dini empress? Are you not the one who destroyed her home and was responsible for the death of her daughters?" Putting a finger up to his lips, the wizard pouted. "Yes, I think you are the very one."

Dorak stopped short.

"The truth hurts, doesn't it, son?" the wizard cracked.

"It was war," Dorak said.

"War is a great excuse for murder and general mayhem. One can kill, plunder, destroy, do things one would not think of doing during peacetime. As long as the term war covers the crimes, it's all right." The wizard sneered at Dorak. "You are such a hypocrite. Even now, you try to hide your sins. You murdered your father, betrayed both of your wives, and disowned your son. Quite an impressive record for such a young man."

"I did what I thought was necessary. The boy is too much like his mother. I took no pleasure in it."

The Black Cacodemon bent down close to Dorak. "It doesn't matter how you feel. It only matters what you do."

"Dorak, do you not see what he is trying to do?" snapped Iegani. "He's trying to demoralize you—make you doubt yourself."

The aga dropped his dagger. Dorak felt sick to his stomach and dropped to the floor, sitting on his haunches. He moaned lowly.

"Get up, Dorak," said Gitar, not without feeling. She felt confused by her simultaneous loathing for the man who had killed her daughters and her need for his support during the present crisis.

Dorak asked, "Do you know what happened to Maura?"

Iegani moved over to Dorak. He shook him violently. "You are not to listen to him. He will lie and cheat us if he has the chance. He is the father of all lies."

"I will be glad to tell him of his lost love," interrupted the wizard, his figure beginning to disappear into the darkness.

"You will say nothing, you black-hearted demon!" Iegani cried.

"Maura died while giving birth to your daughter," said the Black Cacodemon.

Iegani interrupted, "That's not true. I can feel her presence."

"But you have not seen her, have you? You can't make contact with her, Birdman. That's because she is dead," the magician sneered.

"A daughter?" asked Dorak, snapping his head up.

The magician was fading fast into the darkness of the hallway until only his lips could be seen. "Jezra took care of her, if you guess my meaning."

Dorak muffled a cry and felt the floor rushing up to meet him. He had the vague impression someone was laughing, and another person was crying. Then darkness overtook him.

9

Timon awoke before dawn.

He stumbled out of bed and, still half-asleep, pulled on his tunic and leggings. He opened the flap of his tent and daintily stepped outside into the mud, his feet protected by the wooden clogs he had made for this purpose.

The waterboys had already filled everyone's bowl and pitcher for the morning wash.

As a Bhuttanian, Timon preferred to shun all of this excessive grooming, but the empress could smell dirt and body odor ten feet away—and she didn't like it. He didn't see why he had to wash when he was just going to sweat atop a horse anyway.

Resigned, Timon plunged his hands into the icy water and vigorously rubbed his face, neck, and ears, cursing the entire time. With his damp towel, he reached underneath his tunic and wiped his armpits. Satisfied with his ablutions, Timon took a ragged comb and raked the tangles out of his thick, black hair, braiding it into a luxurious tail down his back in Bhuttanian fashion.

Going back into his tent, he wiped his walking boots off with a dirty rag until they were presentable and then pulled them on. Around his forehead, he tied a bright red band. This signified to other hunters not to mistake him for the prey. Going over to a casket, he opened it carefully. The brass casket with its leather hinges had been his father's traveling box where he had kept his personal items. Sifting through the various items, Timon found a small bundle of twigs secured by a leather thong. He selected one and pulled it out.

Timon sifted again through the box and found a precious looking glass encased in brass. Holding up the mirror, Timon took the twig and began cleaning his teeth by rubbing the end of the twig around his gums. Between cleaning, Timon swished his mouth with stale wine and spat it out on the dirt floor of his tent. The scribe took one last glance in the mirror and smiled. His teeth were still presentable, white and straight, even though there were gaps here and there in the back. He did not cover his mouth when he smiled like so many Bhuttanians. His strong teeth were a sign of good health.

Leaving the warm comfort of his tent, Timon hurried to the royal pavilion where he knew the empress would have a breakfast buffet for the hunting party. He was not disappointed when he entered the gaily-decorated tent. In the center of the room, a table groaned from all of the breads, cakes, cheese, and dried fruit placed upon it. Happily, Timon stuffed his pockets with bread. On a wooden plate nicked with use, he piled elegant breakfast cakes the empress liked to eat. If they were good enough for a queen to eat, they were certainly good enough for him. Waiting for the Bhuttanian general, Alexanee, to peruse the table in front of him, Timon finally managed to get to the honey pots where he liberally dabbed honey on his cakes.

Sitting by himself in a quiet corner, Timon gratefully accepted a cup of hot colla tea from a serving lad and contented himself by stuffing his mouth while watching the rest of the party assemble.

The High Priestess of Magi was seated on the dais and giving Rubank a good tongue lashing over something. When anyone walked by, the High Priestess would stop talking and glance surreptitiously around the room. Timon determined she was acting strangely, but thought no more about it, as all of the women from the House of Magi were a strange-acting lot.

One of Maura's lads-in-waiting came from her

private chambers and filled a gold platter with food from the table. Everyone made way for him. Though he was polite, the youth plainly reveled in the fact the much taller and heavier Bhuttanian men made way for him, as did his larger countrywomen. Satisfied his platter was filled with a complete selection for the empress, he nodded to another servant to follow him with a pot of hot colla tea.

Timon wiped crumbs from his mouth with his sleeve. So the empress was going to eat in her private chambers. Thinking that odd, Timon dipped another cake into the pool of honey on his plate and stuffed it into his mouth with relish. Next, he attacked a big slab of orange cheese. With his pocketknife, he cut off the green residue on the outside of the cheese, putting some in his pocket before taking great bites off the chunk left on his plate.

Belching loudly, he apologized to the Hasan Daegian noble women who were seated near him. They nodded their acknowledgment of his apology and began to eat their meal. Watching them, Timon wondered about the prodigious amount of food that had to be provided each day for the army. Not only for the soldiers, but also for their families, visitors, servants, slaves, and laborers who made the camp function, and that did not even include the animals.

Many towns and villages were happy the army moved in their direction as the empress had a reputation of paying for supplies she needed whereas other rulers might have stolen them. Farmers were cash poor and only too happy to see their beet crops taken if they had a little jingle in their pocket after the soldiers left.

Timon shuddered. Who liked beets anyway but Hasan Daegians and peasants? He had to admit the Hasan Daegian cooks had a way with vegetables even the meat-eating Bhuttanians could stomach. Many Bhuttanians were now eating fruits and vegetables of their own accord, even when meat was plentiful.

The young scribe was an astute observer. He could see how the two cultures were subtly blending, even against the wishes of the sterner conservatives from both sides. Timon had to hand it to the empress. She was a visionary. Perhaps she could bring about peace. Roads would be repaired. Roaming bands of thieves and murderers would be imprisoned. Schools would reopen and new ones built. Aqueducts could be constructed and dams erected. His people might even pick up their old nomadic way of life knowing the steppes were safe again.

The young scribe sighed. It was just a pipe dream. The empress would probably be murdered before they reached Bhuttani, and Jezra would reign in her son's name. Timon made a face. Jezra was neither a visionary nor an astute politician. She would bleed the Bhuttanian Empire dry rebuilding Anqara, her beloved razed city.

A gong sounded, and the empress entered the room. All stood.

Maura had donned black leather trousers and a tan twilled shirt under a black leather jacket. Her hair was braided with feathers entwined in the braids. After greeting everyone, she asked about the weather. One of her scouts felt a storm was brewing, and the hunt should be canceled. "Nonsense," snorted Maura. "Royal Scribe, what say you?"

Timon cautiously made his way through the crowd until he was in the immediate circle of the empress. He noticed the scout was scowling at him. "I'm sure your learned women of nature know what is best in matters of weather," he replied. He felt the scout return a kinder gaze in his direction.

"You know this area?"

"Yes, Great Mother. I have hunted here before but as a child."

Acting as though she didn't hear Timon's subtle warning, Maura turned to one of her generals. "Have there been any reports of Jezra's forces in the area?"

General Alexanee shook his head, "No, but that doesn't mean there is no danger."

Choosing to ignore Alexanee's warning as well, Maura declared, "Well, there seems to be nothing to stop me then. If it rains, I will merely take cover the best I can."

The High Priestess broke in, "Servants could follow with a makeshift tent and provisions, Great Mother."

"Thank you, my lady, but we shall have ample provisions. The hunt should take several days," said the empress.

"Yes," Timon replied. "We are going high into the hills to hunt borax. As long as we take guards and provisions in case we don't kill anything to eat, we shall be fine." Timon flinched under the steady gaze of Alexanee, not to mention the Hasan Daegian and Bhuttanian officers.

The Bhuttanian general tried to persuade the empress again. "Let me send in a large party to survey the area."

"And scare the game?" Maura shook her head. "I am bored and am in need of diversion. I want to hunt."

The Hasan Daegian officers, who stood in a little knot, were horrified. Not only was their sovereign leaving the protection of her army, but she was doing so to hunt, an activity they thought a barbaric trait taught to Maura by the Dinii.

Maura pointed to Timon. "He says he has hunted

there plenty of times, and there has never been a problem."

Timon began sweating heavily. He realized if anything happened to the empress, he would be blamed.

Frustrated, General Alexanee clamored, "Great Mother, this is most unreasonable!"

The room became still.

Maura narrowed her eyes into bright slits. "Are you implying I am unreasonable?"

Alexanee lowered his eyes to the floor. "I am sorry, Great Mother, if I gave offense. It is not my intention. I mean only to protect my sovereign from any possible harm."

Maura grabbed a riding crop from a servant, and moving outside the tent, she called over her shoulder. "No offense taken, General. Since you are afraid for my safety, you may accompany me." She tapped the side of her boot impatiently with the quirt.

The general inwardly groaned. He did not want to gallop over the countryside looking for wild borax. He wanted to sleep and make love to his wife, whom he hadn't seen for several years. He was within a few days of his country estate. Instead, he smiled and replied, "Nothing would give me greater pleasure, Great Mother."

"Good. Shall we get started? You there," Maura

said, pointing to Timon. "Do not leave me." She strode outside the tent where horses awaited. Maura mounted a beige Hasan Daegian pony and motioned to the one next to hers. "There, Timon. You shall ride next to me and tell me what you know of the region."

"Great Mother, I am afraid my knowledge has been depleted long ago in our talks," replied Timon, trying not to show his distaste for the small Hasan Daegian pony, unlike the impressive Bhuttanian warhorse. The fact that he was afraid of the giant horses did not enter into his thought processes. All he valued was that a man cut an imposing figure on a Bhuttanian horse while one looked like a fool on the smaller, but tougher Hasan Daegian ponies with one's feet almost dragging the ground.

"Nonsense. You have not even begun to educate me."

"That would be like trying to outshine the sun," teased Timon, holding his breath. He knew the empress disliked empty flattery. Perhaps if she were angry with him, she might command him to stay in the camp.

Maura smiled as though she knew what the royal scribe was trying to manage. "That may be so, but you will try, good scribe, or I will give Rubank a bad report when I return." She spurred her horse and galloped away, leaving Timon and the rest of the hunting party in a flurry of flying clods of dirt.

The Imperial guards immediately started after their empress while a small group of little girls with their woven grass dolls waved goodbye to them.

Alexanee nudged his pony next to Timon. "I do believe Her Majesty expressed her desire you ride with her."

"Yes, General," concurred Timon, not wishing to incur the wrath of this Bhuttanian general, who was already exasperated with this expedition and now with the small horse underneath him. Timon kicked his pony, and it took off following the guards who were already out of sight. He finally joined them several miles across the plain.

The royal scribe was no horseman, but he managed to keep his seat. After several hours, his thigh and calf muscles ached. He wished nothing more than to be in his tent alone and snoring. "Your Majesty, this is where we turn off the main road," he said, reining his horse a hard left. The main road was but a tired little brown scratch on the ground and the path that Timon took was barely perceptible.

Maura signaled to the other horsemen to follow her lead as she turned her horse. She had said little during the journey, as though something weighed heavily on her mind.

Timon regaled Maura with tales of past hunting trips. He told of times when his father had brought him. In the telling, he relived the happy memories of his boyhood and his deceased father.

"You must have loved your father very much," stated Maura.

Timon searched Maura's face to find any hint of mockery. He found only sympathy. "Yes, I did," replied Timon. "He was a great man."

A shadow passed over Maura's face, and she turned away. "No more talk of fathers," she said abruptly, spurring her horse forward.

Confused, Timon slowed the pace of his pony. He wondered if the empress had been close to her father. He decided he did not care about the empress and stopped thinking about her. His mind wandered to past scenes of home when his father had lived, and his mother had been much younger. He remembered the laughter and the love. The recollections warmed Timon's heart, causing him to chuckle.

The hunting party rode a good portion of the day until late afternoon. They came upon a large blue lake nestled at the foot of the Messaad Mountains, which ran northwest of Bhuttani. Scouts had been recruited to monitor for any sign of Jezra's men but found nothing. Mostly, they discovered hill villages deserted for a very long time.

Within her web of protection, Maura watched for signs of borax. Without notice, she would jump from her horse and anxiously push away fallen leaves from the damp earth. If she discovered an animal print, she would smell and taste the dirt forming it. She constantly sniffed the air. Finding spores or droppings, she inhaled their odor. "Several days old" or "a female boaep in heat" Maura would pronounce with authority.

Maura's hunting affectations irritated Timon, as he was exhausted. The sooner he climbed off his wretched little pony, the better he would feel.

The scouts, however, followed behind the empress, study a gnawed branch or scratches on bark, and nod their heads in unison with her decrees.

As if reading Timon's mind, the empress asked Alexanee to make camp near the lake.

The chef immediately raced ahead to stake out a suitable spot where she could cook for the empress and her party.

Alexanee reigned in his horse, sighing with relief. He assigned guards around the campsite and sent several men on ahead to stand watch in the hills. Hasan Daegian women guarded the empress while the Bhuttanian men took the outer perimeters of the camp.

Stiff from the ride, Maura jumped off her pony and stretched. She informed her guards she was going to bathe in the lake. Shedding her sweaty hunting clothes, Maura was clad only in her undergarments with a dagger hidden in her shirtwaist. Diving into the water, the empress found it bracing. She stayed only long enough to wash the dirt and sweat off. Upon her return to shore, she found a warm towel, fresh clothes, and soft sandals, which she donned with pleasure. It was good to be out of that tight leather.

Maura hurried over to the campfire where she discovered Timon sitting near the flames with his feet immersed in a bucket of hot water.

Timon immediately tried to stand.

Maura bid him and the rest of the officers to remain seated. "Feet hurt, Timon?" inquired Maura.

"Great Mother, I am not accustomed to riding a horse this long. I usually walk."

"Then I would think another part of your anatomy would be affected."

"That hurts as well, Great Mother." Timon grinned sheepishly. "I guess I am not much of a horseman even though I am Bhuttanian."

"Do you know of this lake?" asked Maura, changing the subject.

"Yes, Great Mother. It is called the Lake of Forgotten Dreams."

"Why is that?"

"It is said a person who has a deep and abiding regret can come here, drink of the cool waters, and forget. Thus the Lake of Forgotten Dreams."

"I wish life's decisions could be that easily forgotten," interjected Alexanee. He had grown up with silly stories about this lake and wished Timon would be quiet. This part of the Bhuttanian Empire made him uneasy with its eerie silence and strange shadows.

The empress joked, "If that be true, we should all drink buckets full."

Everyone laughed heartily except for Timon and Alexanee, who watched the remaining swath of sunlight turn the water into a fiery haze. Night fell quickly in the forest, and as soon as Maura had eaten, she bid her company goodnight and retired to her tent.

Timon followed the empress' example and turned in early. As soon as his head hit his saddle, he fell into a deep sleep, unlike the empress who tossed and turned in her tent.

Unable to rest, Maura sat up and swung her sturdy legs over the cot. She wiped the sweat from her brow and tasted it. It tasted of fear. "Please, Mekonia, do not let me fail tomorrow," she whispered before falling into a dreamless state that vaguely resembled death.

10

The empress rose.

She called to her uultepes. They had been sleeping in tree limbs overhanging Maura's tent and sprang down upon hearing her voice. Purring, they entered her tent and sat obediently in front of their mistress. If one chanced upon this sight, she would swear the woman and the cats stared at each other as if they were playing a peek-a-boo game and nothing more passed between them, but a wise person would know better.

The uultepes followed Maura out of the tent and immediately went over to a tree for the express purpose of sharpening their claws. They would stop now and then to inspect their razor sharp nails. Satisfied, they licked them clean until light reflected off of them.

The sound of the uultepes ripping bark off the trees caused Timon to groggily raise his head to see what was causing the fuss. He sneered at the menacing beasts.

Aware they were being watched, the uultepes stopped their grooming.

Timon swallowed hard. He would have sworn to a priest in a sacred oath the uultepes smiled at him. It lasted only for a few seconds before they returned to scratching the tree, but he was convinced they had actually smiled, and the smiles were not kind. Timon jumped up from his bedroll and stumbled away, nearly running into General Alexanee.

"The latrine is that way, boy."

Sheepishly, Timon followed the general's thumb toward the latrine. He nearly stumbled into the hastily dug hole in the ground. As he relieved himself, he glanced up into the trees and choked. One of the uultepes sat watching him. Timon spat at the fearsome cat. "Get away, you spawn of a demon," hissed Timon, pulling his tunic down.

Startled it had been discovered, the cat jumped down and hurried out of sight.

Before Timon had time to compose himself, several guards joined him, hastily removing their codpieces. They sighed in unison. Timon wasn't sure if the chorus of sighs was due to their relief at being off duty or emptying their bladders. Timon left the guards still sighing and realized he was hungry. He washed in haste at the lake's shore, rebraided his hair, and then made his way to the cook's wagon. Mush and day-old sweetbread was served along with hot colla tea. He waited patiently as the senior officers filled their plates and stuffed their pockets before he got in line.

As he ate, Timon checked the sky. It looked dark, as though a storm brewed in the west. Clouds threatened the sky, and the treetops bent in the strengthening breezes. Catching the eye of General Alexanee, Timon winced. He, too, had been checking the atmospheric conditions. His stony glare at Timon only convinced the youth the general held him responsible for the coming bad weather. Losing his appetite, Timon inwardly groaned as he watched the general head toward the empress' tent. He prayed to the nameless god of Anqara that Alexanee get his way, and the hunting party return to the army.

Several minutes later, Alexanee stormed out, running his hands through his thick hair. He sat grumpily on a stump, snapping at his servant to comb his hair. When his grooming was finished, Alexanee stood and called out, "We hunt today. Saddle your horses. Be quick about it. She wants to leave before the storm hits." Everyone scurried to the horses as the servants broke camp. Striding over to Timon, Alexanee puffed heavily, "Scribe, Her Majesty wants you to ride beside her at all times." The general grabbed Timon's arm. "Nothing had better go wrong."

Knowing a warning when he heard one, Timon nodded as one struck dumb. He knew if any unpleasantness befell the empress, Alexanee would make him the scapegoat. Timon braced himself mentally. Nothing should happen. Nothing must happen!

The empress strode out of her tent dressed in a forest green hunting outfit. She carried a Hasan Daegian bow and a quiver filled with Hasan Daegian style arrows. Her dark hair fell loose about her shoulders and blew gently in the breeze. For once, Timon thought Maura looked young.

The empress mounted her pony and smiled expectantly at Timon. "Lead the way, young man," she commanded softly.

Realizing she was speaking to him, Timon stiffly mounted his pony and led the way up a path, which would eventually open to a field where wild borax often grazed in the soft early morning light.

Maura signaled for only a few guards to follow her. She did not want the game to be frightened away by the trampling of too many horses.

After an hour of rigorous travel, the small party finally emerged into a soft meadow where a small herd of borax grazed quietly. The animals immediately became alarmed at the arrival of the hunting party. Massive heads lifted from the grass as the borax began snorting and pawing the ground. Large pointed spikes emerged from the humps on their backs, which ran from the tip of their heads down their spines while their shaggy heads brandished an impressive set of horns.

Maura was surprised at the immense size of the wild borax and momentarily cautious. She had seen only domestic borax, which had purposely been bred smaller. She whistled to Timon and motioned that he was to circle on the outside of the meadow until he reached the opposite side to await her signal.

Timon moved his pony along the outskirts as Maura walked her pony in the opposite direction.

Slowly pulling out an arrow, she notched it in her bow, guiding her pony with only her knees while holding the reins in her mouth. She placed the bow into a striking position, her arm expertly cocked and right eye centered on the largest bull in the herd. Giving out a loud war cry, Maura urged her pony into the midst of the herd.

Guessing this must be the signal, Timon kicked his horse forward and ran at the herd causing it to split. Timon hung onto his pony as best he could, realizing he would be trampled to death if he fell off.

The borax scattered, running in confused circles.

Bellowing loudly, many borax charged Timon's pony, but he deftly managed to outmaneuver them. From the corner of his eye, he spied Maura shooting an arrow into the large bull, which enraged the animal into a bitter fury. Her horse circled around the animal as Maura notched another arrow and took aim. The bull, bleeding from his shoulder, charged Maura with surprising speed and rammed her pony. Maura's arrow shot upward, missing its mark. Before she could replace the arrow, the borax rammed the pony again, causing it to stumble. This gave the bull the time it needed to lower its head and slam into the pony with its spiny head.

Jumping off, Maura hit the ground, rolling away from her fallen pony. Satisfied the pony was no longer a threat, the bull skirted to the other side where Maura was and charged. Seeing Timon was too far away to help, Maura picked up her fallen quiver and bow and ran into the woods with the bull in full pursuit.

Timon's worst fears had been realized. The empress was now running for her life from an enraged borax bull that would undoubtedly gore her to death.

Knowing his life would be forfeited if that happened, Timon whipped the neck of his pony with his leather reins, spurring the animal after the fleeing empress. Acting on instinct, Timon drew his hunting sword from its scabbard as he raced into the woods. Ducking branches, he was momentarily blinded by stinging twigs slapping his face. Feeling wetness on his brow and cheeks, he realized his face was bleeding. He pushed that concern aside. Wiping blood from his eyes, Timon urged his pony deeper into the dense forest, but the pony pulled up and pranced nervously.

Timon looked about him. He had lost sight of the empress. He twisted in his saddle, turning his head in every direction listening, hoping to catch the sounds of the borax, only to hear a scream coming from the right. "Oh, Nameless One, let it not be so!" he cried as he pushed his pony into the dense foliage. He rode forward using his arms to protect his face from treacherous briars striking him.

He rode into a small clearing where he spied the empress. At her feet lay the borax bull being disemboweled by one of her uultepes.

Maura looked at him as Timon entered the clearing, pulling up his horse. Her face was drained of color.

Timon was reminded of an animated death mask. Suddenly, Timon was knocked out of his saddle and hit the ground with a heavy thud. Trying to rise, Timon felt a strong hand push his face toward the ground.

Someone pulled Timon up to his knees and stuck a rag into his mouth. Before Timon could fight back, his arms were quickly bound. He blindly kicked, causing him to fall forward.

Feeling vomit move up his throat, Timon gagged on the cloth in his mouth. Momentarily closing his eyes, Timon tried to focus on what was happening, but he didn't have time.

Something screamed, and it sounded human.

Timon snapped his eyes open and searched for the empress. He saw her standing near the borax.

She was drenched in blood.

Before her lay an unconscious man dressed exactly as himself. Maura uttered to the man, "I am sorry." With that, she signaled to the uultepes sitting atop of the carcass of the dead borax.

A uultepe sprang forward and effortlessly crushed the man's thorax with its massive teeth.

Death was swift.

Sensing its prey was dead, the uultepe took its claws and raked the face of its victim.

Timon moaned, turning his head away. Almost senseless, he felt himself being lifted and thrown over a saddle—a Bhuttanian warhorse saddle. He was tied to the horse. The horse shifted its weight, causing the ropes to cut into Timon's flesh.

"Hurry," he heard Maura say.

Someone else grunted in reply.

Maura pulled Timon's head up by his hair and peered anxiously into his face.

Timon slowly opened his eyes.

"You had to be the one," she whispered. "There was no one else." Her face swirled before Timon as he tried to pull his head out of her grasp. Gently, Maura kissed him. "Good luck to you, Royal Scribe."

"We must be off," a man grunted.

Timon could feel Maura's breasts brush against him as she checked the ropes binding him. Soft leather was inserted between his skin and the ropes.

"There is no time for that," barked the man. "Give it to me, and I'll be off!"

Maura tore the amulet from her neck and placed it into the man's outstretched hand. "Take care," she said, slapping his horse on the rump.

The man rode off, leading Timon's horse into the dense forest.

Hearing her guards calling, Maura broke off a leafy branch, wiping out the man's tracks. Satisfied, she ran over to the fallen borax and scooted herself under its heavy hooves.

When the guards came upon the clearing, they found their empress unconscious—just the way she had planned.

11

Timon was oblivious to time.

He did not know if it was night or day. The gag was removed, and he was given water occasionally. Timon's left eye was swollen shut, and he spat blood when he wasn't drifting in and out of consciousness. Finally, he felt the horse jolt to a stop. Several pairs of hands undid his bindings, easing him gently to the ground. His hands and feet were freed. Timon tried to open his good eye, but a blinding sun blotted out everything with its yellow brightness. Cool hands wiped his brow while another pair of hands removed his clothes.

In other circumstances, Timon would have struggled, but he lay passively, grateful the unseen hands were gentle on his burning skin. He heard a woman say, "He is awfully bruised. He will need rest and tending."

A man replied, "There wasn't enough time to treat

him like a baby. He put up more of a struggle than I thought he would. I had to get him out of there before one of those damn cats attacked him."

"The empress?"

There was a pause before the man spoke. "It does not matter if she was hurt. She can heal herself."

"I wasn't talking about her body."

"She is more Dinii than she is Hasan Daegian. Her practical nature will see her through this."

"Her true nature is that of a Hasan Daegian. She will struggle with this."

"That's her problem. The man was an animal who murdered women and children for pleasure. He was scheduled to be executed anyway."

The woman sighed. "I suppose."

Timon's head was tilted back, and small fingers pried open his mouth.

"This will help you to sleep the rest of the way," Timon heard a woman say.

Timon obediently drank a bitter draught. He fell into a deep sleep and did not open his eyes again until he was jostled awake. He realized he was in a wagon struggling to get its wheels over a deep rut in the road.

A woman bent over him, peering anxiously into his face.

For a brief second Timon thought he recognized

her, but the thought swiftly fled, leaving him confused.

The woman patted his shoulder. "Go back to sleep," she said softly. "We are not there yet." Timon did as the woman commanded and fell back to sleep.

12

Birds twittered happily.

A stream gurgled like a laughing child. Horses snorted contently grazing on thick grass.

Timon sat up straight. Still groggy, he looked about with half-opened eyes. He was in a well-made traveling wagon with all of the comforts of a nobleman. Timon pushed a warm coverlet off. He was naked except for oils and herbs covering his body in a thick poultice. Timon realized someone had cared well for him.

Feeling his bladder threatening to burst, Timon struggled to get up. His hands fumbled upon a container left by his bed for that purpose. Timon used the vessel, anxious that it might spill over, but its contents came right to the rim and no farther. Timon studied his urine and smelled it. It was a pale green and possessed an acrid odor.

"I will take that," said a female voice.

Timon's head jerked upward.

"Don't be embarrassed. I am a healer." The woman took the filled vessel from Timon's hands. She smelled the urine without hesitation and tasted a drop of it from her finger before handing it to someone outside the wagon. She smiled tenderly at Timon. "I need to examine you. It will only take a moment, and then you may dress if you like." She knelt down beside his pallet and with quick, efficient hands, the healer examined Timon's body, even checking his ears and throat. She leaned her head against his chest and counted his heartbeats. Satisfied with his recovery, she smiled.

"I know you."

"I am flattered you remember."

"Why have I been abducted, Lady Pearl?"

"Why indeed?" said KiKu, entering the wagon. "I see you have recovered with my wife's help."

"She has taken admirable care of me, but I wonder for what purpose?" Timon tried not to show fear at the sight of KiKu.

KiKu gave his wife a knowing look.

She rose and left the wagon, leaving them alone.

KiKu sat down on a stool. "Your clothes are over there," he declared, pointing to several robes hanging on wall pegs.

"Those clothes are too costly for a mere scribe."

KiKu smiled. "There is no need for subterfuge anymore, Prince Bes Amon Ptah. You must have forgotten I was in attendance at Zoar's court when your father first brought you with your older brother. I could not forget such frightened boys, who were pledged as collateral for your father's good behavior. You see, the same thing happened to my sister and myself."

"I don't know what you are talking about," replied Timon stubbornly.

"Yes, you do, but I will refer to you as Timon, if you wish it. I will wait for you outside. Please hurry. There is much to discuss." KiKu left.

KiKu's two youngest wives entered with towels and a tub of warm water. "Do you wish assistance with bathing, Prince Bes?" asked Tippu. "It would be both our pleasure and honor to help you." Tippu giggled behind her tiny hand.

Unhappily, Timon shook his head. "My name is Timon."

"Perhaps we can help you to stand?"

"Yes," answered Timon, extending his arm. "I am a little unsteady on my feet."

Tippa brought over a chair and turned its back toward Timon. "Use this to steady yourself. We will wait just outside in case you call."

"You are most kind," replied Timon sincerely.

The twins bowed and left the wagon.

Timon heard them chatter excitedly near the door while pulling himself up using the chair. He bathed slowly and dressed in the fine undergarments left for him.

Still woozy, he called for the twins, and they finished dressing him. Tenderly, they massaged Timon's head and combed the tangles out of his freshly washed hair. Tippa shaved him after rubbing fine oils into his skin. Soft leather slippers were placed on his feet and costly earrings on his lobes. After their skillful ministrations, Timon felt that he could function and made his way out of the wagon, carefully stepping down the worn painted steps.

The sun was waning, and KiKu, with his first two wives, was studying its descent over the mountains. "Ah, you truly look like a prince now," said KiKu admiringly. He motioned for a servant to bring a traveling chair for the prince.

Still weak, Timon sat. He gratefully accepted food from another servant. Timon hesitated a moment before eating.

"It is not poisoned," reassured KiKu. To show Timon the food wasn't tainted, KiKu stole a morsel from the plate and ate it.

Timon appeared unimpressed. "Why am I here?"

"That will take some explaining."

"I have nothing but time."

"That is precisely what you don't have."

There was no need for pretense now. KiKu had remembered him. Timon took stock of his abductor. "Are you threatening me?"

A deep laugh rose from KiKu's belly. "No, Prince Bes. I am merely stating a fact. I will start at the beginning. Please hold your questions until I finish." KiKu shifted his weight to a more comfortable position. "Have you ever heard of the Lahorians?"

Timon shook his head.

"The Lahorians are the reason you are here, my friend. Many generations ago, when the Dinii were the Overlords of our world, Kaseri—when your Bhuttanian ancestors were just another poor nomadic tribe roaming the steppes, when my people were just beginning to coalesce into a nation, a people from another world came to live on islands off the shores of Hasan Daeg. We called them the Lahorians. The Lahorians were truth seekers, wishing only to evolve until they joined the Great Truth."

"What truth is that?" interrupted Timon.

KiKu shrugged. "Who knows what they mean? Perhaps they mean the Creator. The important thing is they came here seeking a place to live. A great flood occurred, covering the islands on which they lived and causing the Lahorians to escape to the closest high land. Unfortunately, they ended upon land, which was the Dinii's territory. As natural predators, the Dinii immediately tried to conquer the desperate Lahorians and subjugate them.

"But the Lahorians possessed great power and were not easily defeated. A terrible war ensued. There was much loss of life and destruction on both sides. Realizing they could not conquer the Lahorians, the Dinii fled to Hasan Daeg, taking their slaves with them.

"The war was cataclysmic for the Dinii culture. They had lost everything, even their confidence, their sense of self. So shaken were they, the Dinii pretended that the war had never occurred. Future generations were not taught of their history except for only a few nobles. Within a few generations, the knowledge died away, and the existence of the Lahorians was forgotten."

"But the Lahorians survived?"

"Yes, well enough they could propagate their species and carry out their original mission."

"Which was?"

"As I explained before—to follow their destiny and join with Truth," KiKu replied.

"Uh-huh."

"By your expression, Prince Bes—I mean Timon—I don't think you believe me. It is indeed a wondrous tale."

"Fantasy is a better word. My mother told me fairy stories that were more believable."

"I don't blame you, but I know it to be true. I have seen the Lahorians and their magnificent underwater city. The story is no more ridiculous than that of a young prince, known only to a few, hidden away in the recesses of the Zoar's palace as a royal hostage. A prince who decides to take advantage of Zoar's death to hide, so he may one day escape back to the Steppes of Moab. But fate takes a cruel hand. He is hustled into the Bhuttanian army by those unaware of his identity and spends years wasting away as a lowly bureaucrat. Finally, he gets close to his home again only to be chosen by the royal consul to become his personal scribe. Now his every moment is accounted for, and he cannot slip away in the night without having the Imperial guards after him by morning's light."

The scribe did not know how to respond. It was useless to deny his identity any longer.

Kiku continued with his eyes burning into Timon. "I was hoping to impress upon you the importance of our mission, but I will explain things in a more mundane fashion for your benefit." KiKu reached for a small scroll inside his vest and handed it to Timon. "You are to journey to the temple of Bhuttu where you will apply for training as a votary. There you will seek to discover the meaning of sightings by the priests."

"What sightings?"

"There are rumors the Dinii have been seen by the priests. You are to confirm any sightings and do whatever you must to free the Dinii."

Timon refused to take the scroll from KiKu. "I am not a spy. I am not a soldier. I have no idea of how to proceed in such matters. What you ask is impossible. I won't do it." Timon pressed his lips together into a tight thin line, allowing his eyes to brighten with defiance.

KiKu rose and dropped the scroll at Timon's feet. "Then your mother, your sisters, their husbands, and children will be tortured and killed. Every living animal your people possess will be confiscated so they may starve to death."

Jumping to his feet as a man released from a paralyzing dream, Timon struck KiKu with his fists, putting the full force of his body behind him. KiKu let Timon hit him several times and then expertly grabbed his arms. Like lightning, KiKu twisted Timon around, choking the young man. Try as he may, Timon could not get KiKu to release his hold from around his neck. KiKu squeezed tighter until Timon struggled no more.

KiKu whispered into the boy's ear. "Take my advice, young cub. Take up the struggle and join the rest of us who are fighting to preserve life on this planet. Are you forever going to hide among those eunuch scribes like a coward?" KiKu released the gasping prince.

Wiping blood from his mouth, KiKu sneered in contempt at Timon struggling to rise from the ground. "Perhaps the empress was wrong about you. She said you were untested clay who could be molded into a man of courage and tenacity." KiKu roared, "I SEE NO SUCH MAN HERE!"

Timon's face was clouded with pain and doubt. "I am not a coward!"

"I am not the one on my knees with my balls hanging out of my clothes like some boy whore in the back streets of Bhuttani." KiKu kicked the scroll over to Timon. "Read the scroll. If by morning you do not willingly assume your task, I will send word of your refusal to the empress."

"You can't do that. My people will die!"

KiKu spoke in soft tones. "Yes. They will die, but you will exist many years so you may live with your shame and guilt each day. You will be disgraced, a man without family or friend or tribe. All will curse your name and shun your company. No one fails Maura without a sorrowful price to pay."

"Then I have no choice," said Timon bitterly.

"You have a choice. You may take up the sword and fight, possibly dying like a man, or you can let your kin die a terrible death by saving your own skin. But let me tell you one thing, my friend, you will never be allowed to commit suicide if that occurs. You will be forced to live with your terrible pain the rest of your natural life." KiKu's voice dripped with disgust. "I told the empress you would be useless. Even the Hasan Daegian men, as small and effeminate as they are, fight like demons to protect their own. No one has to threaten them to put down their painted fans and pick up a sword." KiKu began to walk away.

"KIKU!" cried out Timon. "I am afraid."

KiKu turned and studied Timon for a moment. "So am I, Prince Bes. I sweat with fear every night, but in the morning, I face whatever the day brings. There is no shame in my heart. Good night, Prince Bes." KiKu's wives followed him with their heads bent down.

Timon wiped away tears staining his face. He struggled to his feet to make his way back to the wagon when he stepped on the scroll. Gingerly, he picked up the dirt-smeared parchment. Allowing one of KiKu's servants to escort him to the wagon, Timon did not resist when the man helped him out of his fine clothes.

Timon rested on his bed. "Bring the lamp over to me, then leave," ordered Timon. The servant quickly left after handing the lamp to the young prince.

With trembling hands, Timon broke the Royal Hasan Daegian and Bhuttanian Imperial seals and unrolled the parchment. He scanned the writing quickly, trying to comprehend every word.

Prince Bes Amon Ptah,

You will be reading this after several intense days. Your feelings may range anywhere from anger to surprise to fear. Everything that has happened was necessary, I assure you.

The hunt was a ruse to stage your death. A convict with your coloring and body build was selected to switch places with you. Everyone had to be convinced you were dead. I could not take a chance that your people would look for you if you were thought to be missing.

I have known who you are for a long time. You have been under surveillance, as have other noble hostages of Zoar. Rubank thought it most ingenious of you to hide among the scribe guild. He thought your resourcefulness most impressive. Of course, KiKu confirmed your identity when he saw you at my court.

I have a mission for you. You are to proceed to the temple of Bhuttu posing as a nobleman's son seeking entrance as a novice. KiKu and his wives are to pose as your servants. Once there, you are to confirm reports of any unnatural sightings in the temple. I am hoping you will send word that you have sighted the Dinii. If you do confirm the Dinii are hidden away in the temple, you are to use whatever means possible to free them. There is a possibility that they have been bound by magic.

KiKu and his family have pledged their lives to protect you. If they fail, they will die. If you fail, your family will die.

It is a harsh edict, so leave no stone unturned. I wait for your successful return.

Maura de Magela

Timon burned the scroll in the lamp. Grabbing a robe, he hurried to KiKu's wagon. "KiKu, let me enter," Timon called out.

One of the twins opened the door and bade the Prince to enter. KiKu was in a dressing gown lounging on cushions with his wives. He seemed surprised to see Timon so soon after their confrontation.

"I thought you had retired. You must take care not to tax yourself," Pearl cautioned.

"You did not tell me your life would be forfeited if I refused. Would she really do that to you? I thought you had saved her life," blurted Timon.

"If by 'she' you mean the empress, yes. She is not in

the position to do as she wants, but as she must. That is what you do not understand. Do you think she wanted to kill that man in the meadow? She didn't have a choice in the matter. She is trying to locate the Dinii, powerful allies, who will save thousands of lives if they fight with her again. She is trying to overturn an ancient feudal system, which has left much of our world in tattered rags with half of its people dying from starvation and poisoned water. In that context, what is the consequence of one life such as mine or even yours?

"You stand there self-righteous and condemning, but you have been a bystander for years hiding away while others have made the hard choices. She does not have the luxury of worrying about morality. She must be practical and cunning or all will be lost."

Madric interrupted, "Tell us, Timon, which queen will serve the Empire better, Maura or Jezra? You were at court with Jezra. You have spent more than a year with Maura. Which one would you chose?"

Timon did not know how to respond. Wasn't Maura like any other ruler—cruel with an impossible obsession for power?

KiKu sighed at Timon's lack of insight. "Let's start with the obvious," said KiKu, looking to his oldest wife for support. "Maura is uniting two vastly different cultures that had been warring with each other only years ago. Why do you think it is taking the army years to reach Bhuttani? She wanted time to unit the Hasan Daegians and Bhuttanians into one people. Jezra could never have achieved this. Jezra would not even see the need to do so."

"You must realize Jezra is just a woman, but Maura is a true queen," Pearl interjected.

"And you are willing to die for her?" questioned Timon.

KiKu's voice quivered with emotion. "I am willing to die for what she believes in, for it is the same as I believe."

Timon held out his hands. "That's my problem. I don't believe in anything."

"But you do, Timon," said Pearl. "You believe in love for your mother and your family. You believe in your people. It is a beginning."

"It does not matter what he believes in," snapped KiKu at his wife. "Maura has removed all political and religious obstacles from your path. She is using the oldest of all persuasions—fear. If you do not go to Bhuttani and fulfill your mission, those you love most in the world will die a terrible death. You can live a coward's life, or you may try to save them. As it is, they are dead already, practically speaking. She is giving you a chance to bring them back from the hall of death," admonished KiKu, pounding his fist in his hand, "and it can be done!"

Timon spat, "I will go to Bhuttani and do as you ask. I will tell you with all honesty I think this is a fool's errand."

KiKu's face split into a sadistic grin. "A fool can be the most dangerous enemy of all."

13

Alexanee pulled off the shroud.

He examined the torn and tattered remains carefully. A Bhuttanian healer stood in the corner anxiously watching. "Tell me something I don't already know," requested Alexanee, peering hopefully at the healer.

The healer stepped forward into the light. He replied, "Wounds were caused by claws. The boy's throat was crushed by an animal."

"He suffocated?"

The healer shrugged. "Whether he bled to death or suffocated is only a matter of seconds." He waved his hand over the shredded body. "There was not much with which to work."

"What kind of animal?"

The healer glanced up in surprise at Alexanee's frowning face. "The uultepes, of course."

"It couldn't have been the borax?"

"No, General Alexanee. If it had been the borax, the body would have broad puncture wounds from the borax goring with his horns. A borax cannot cause this kind of damage to the throat. No, this was the work of a powerful predator."

Alexanee pondered for a moment.

"If I may be so bold, General Alexanee, I have seen the work of the uultepes before. This is their doing."

"Is there anything unique about this attack?"

The healer smiled—several of his front teeth were missing. "Yes, my lord. This goes beyond what a uultepe would need to do in order to kill its victim, even if it was a fierce confrontation."

Alexanee went over to the carcass of the borax and squatted beside it. "What can you tell me about this animal?"

"It was a male bull in its prime weighing about three thousand pounds. Death was caused by a crushed thorax as well." The healer pulled back hanging skin to expose a gaping wound.

"What about all of these claw marks?" asked Alexanee, pointing to the rows of long rakes on the body.

"They were made after the animal was dead."

"Really!"

The healer puffed up his chest with pride. He could

hardly believe he was talking to the exalted Alexanee as an equal. "You can see, General Alexanee, there is hardly any blood from these wounds. That would indicate this damage was done after the heart had stopped beating."

Alexanee stood and rubbed his chin. "Where are the clothes of the man?"

The healer called for a servant, who brought a bundle of bloody rags. Alexanee took the bundle.

Unlike his master, the servant was only too happy to leave the general. He did not like being so close to a noble who could have him put to death on a whim.

Alexanee, oblivious to the servant's consternation, patiently sifted through the remains of a tunic, gloves, leggings, a loincloth, and gnawed hunting boots. "Is this everything?"

The healer nodded. "This is everything on him except for the boots. They were knocked off his feet during the attack, I guess." The healer shuddered. "I imagine he did not suffer very long. He probably went into shock at the beginning of the attack and knew nothing after that." The healer glanced down at the shredded rags and let out a low whistle.

"There is nothing else?"

Curiously, the healer replied, "No, my lord."

"There was no red hunting headband?"

"No, my lord."

"You would stake your life on it?"

The healer's eyes grew wide into startled pools. "Yes, my lord. There was no red hunting headband when this man was brought in. I saw to the remains alone. No one else has been near him or his clothes."

"What about your servants?"

The healer shifted his large frame uneasily. He did not like being questioned about the honor of his household. The healer was a proud man and was known for his competence. "I can vouch for all of my servants. No one had access to this body except for me and my assistant, whom you just saw. He has been with me for twenty years. I trust him completely. He cannot be bribed."

Alexanee grunted with satisfaction.

The healer grunted in reply, as was the Bhuttanian custom.

"Is this the body of the scribe Timon?"

The healer pondered the implications of the question. He spoke cautiously. "The body is the same height and weight of the royal scribe. Hair is the same as any Bhuttanian boy. This is the remains of a young Bhuttanian male with nomadic breeding, but . . ." the healer paused.

"But what?"

"His face was obliterated during the attack. The skin and cartilage have been shredded. The eyes destroyed. Without a face, there is no way I can be positive." The healer folded his arms and rocked back on his heels. "This reminds me of something."

Alexanee waited patiently.

"I was one of the physicians attending the Aga Dorak during the siege of O Konya. The night the empress made her escape, there was a terrible battle in the palace. Some of the Bhuttanian soldiers killed had their faces disfigured."

"That is correct," affirmed Alexanee.

"The faces of the Bhuttanian soldiers were ravaged by dagger cuts, and a few had their noses sliced off."

Alexanee closed his eyes for a moment. "I remember. We were tearing the city apart trying to find the empress. None of the soldiers in the city were disfigured. Just those in the palace."

"I had always thought it strange the Hasan Daegians were so vicious that night. They had never desecrated an enemy soldier before. They had always been respectful of our dead. It was unlike them." The healer thought how ironic life was. The woman, who had been hunted like an animal that awful night, now commanded them and, with one word, could have them all hung.

Alexanee cleared his throat.

Realizing he had drifted, the healer snapped to attention and bowed low. "Is there anything else I can do for you, General Alexanee?"

Alexanee pressed gold coins into the healer's hands. "I don't need to tell you that our conversation is private. I want nothing said of this. No report."

Without searching the general's penetrating dark eyes, the healer lowered his head in acceptance.

Alexanee grunted, "Good. I am sure we understand each other. I am pleased with your work. You may resume your duties now."

The general returned to his tent, happy to be away from that dreadful sight. He sat on his cot thinking for a very long time before a servant entered, bringing a lamp and a tray of food.

Alexanee glanced up in surprise. "Is it night?"

"In a very short while, my lord," assured the servant. "There is still enough daylight to walk the camp without a torch."

The general stood at the entrance of his tent, thinking.

After finding the empress under the hooves of the borax, the hunting party had returned posthaste to the encampment, while Alexanee and several of his men had remained scouting the area and waiting for wagons in which to retrieve the bodies of the dead scribe and the borax. Since returning, he had not even changed his offensive clothing but waited for the healer to examine the bodies. Realizing he stank, Alexanee called for a hot bath and gave his clothes to the servant to burn.

Seeing the servant's face flicker before returning to its usual stoic reserve, Alexanee hid his smile, also. Even the servants were taking on the Hasan Daegian custom of bathing. He pondered the blending of the Bhuttanian and Hasan Daegian cultures. He was no fool. He could see what the empress was trying to achieve with subtle machinations here and there.

Alexanee wondered what his fellow officers would think if they could see him relaxing in a wooden tub filled with bubbling water as his feet stuck precariously over the edge. His keen mind raced with a thousand different thoughts, but like threads of lightning springing from the same thundercloud, they merged into one mighty bolt of light—the lifeless body of the Bhuttanian male waiting for cremation was not the royal scribe, Timon!

The empress had made one mistake. Where was the red hunting band Timon had worn when he chased after the Maura and the charging borax? It should have been with the body. His men had retraced Timon's steps, and not even a shred of red material could be found. Even the dead boy's mouth had been examined, as well as the contents of his stomach and those of the borax. Perhaps the uultepes had swallowed the headband during the attack? By now, the fierce cat-like animals should have passed anything in their system. Alexanee's men had found nothing while searching their droppings. Why was the headband missing and where was it?

The tall and powerfully built Alexanee pounded his chest, hoping to relieve the anxiety he felt. In doing so, dirty water splashed over the sides of the tub, falling in great pools spreading on the carpeted ground. What was the inscrutable Maura up to? The general closed his eyes and slid deeper into the warm water, only to rise from his bath when the water cooled. Calling a servant to help, Alexanee dressed hurriedly and followed a guide bearing a torch, leading him through the camp to the empress' tent. Without hesitation, Maura's servants granted General Alexanee admission into her private chamber.

Looking pale and weak, the empress lay propped up by pillows on her bed. Near her side stood the High Priestess from the House of Magi and personal physician, Meagan of Skujpor, who was taking the empress' pulse.

Alexanee had to quell an impulse to laugh. If anyone didn't need a healer, it was Maura de Magela. Even at the site of the hunting accident, he didn't think she needed much medical attention.

"Great Mother," said Alexanee, bowing very low.

Maura waved him closer to her bed with a slight move of a finger.

The High Priestess slinked into the dark shadows of the room until she was almost invisible.

"I see you have made a safe return, General Alexanee," uttered the empress in a small voice.

"I am distressed that you have taken to your bed, Great Mother."

Maura ignored the small hint of sarcasm in the general's voice. "I am grateful I have not suffered any major injuries."

"As we all are."

"It is the shock of seeing young Timon torn so." She closed her eyes. "It has unsettled me. I feel so responsible."

"I understand, Great Mother. No one likes to see such a young life taken in such a manner."

Maura's dark eyes snapped open. "What manner would that be, General Alexanee?"

Meagan of Skujpor pulled the blanket higher around Maura's waist as one might tuck a child into bed. She gave a warning look to Alexanee as not to tire the empress with questions.

"I was wondering, Great Mother, if you happened to pick up the red headband of the boy during the struggle or perhaps it got caught on your boots?"

"Why do you ask?"

"Timon's hunting band is missing. I can't find it anywhere."

"I'm afraid I don't remember much of the attack. I do know Timon's horse was gored by the borax, causing Timon to fall. Then the borax turned on me, and I saw Timon running toward me. I fell beneath the borax, and that is all I remember." Maura winced as in pain.

Alexanee continued, refusing to acknowledge Maura's implied pain. "Timon's body had many deep cuts, apparently caused by an animal with sharp claws, not hooves. Do you think—in all the excitement—the uultepes could have attacked him by mistake?"

"Are you implying the borax did not kill Timon?"

"No, Great Mother, it is just his face has been erased, so to speak. I don't think even a borax could have caused such damage."

"It is possible the uultepes could have mistaken Timon for an attacker."

Alexanee grunted. "Do you think Timon could have been trying to attack you?"

"I think Timon an improbable choice for an assassin, but as I have said before, I don't know what happened. I hit my head when I fell underneath the borax and blacked out."

A lad-in-waiting carried over to General Alexanee a carved box and laid it at his feet. Alexanee hesitated.

"Allow me, General," offered Meagan of Skujpor, knowing Bhuttanians dislike for opening strange boxes or trunks. More than one Bhuttanian had been killed by opening a booby-trapped receptacle. She untied the leather straps holding the box closed. Carefully, she opened the lid. "I saved all of her Majesty's clothes for your inspection. I knew you would want to make a full report to the Council of Nobles."

Alexanee grunted.

Meagan grunted using the female Bhuttanian response of two sounds instead of one. She pulled out the empress' tattered green hunting outfit. The pants were split up the back and on the left side. The shirt was covered in blood, but otherwise seemed in good shape except for the right sleeve, which had been completely severed.

Alexanee examined the clothes closely and smelled them. They had a female musk odor to them that could not be obliterated by the smell of dried blood and dirt. For a second, Alexanee thought of his wife, who was waiting impatiently for him in their warm and cozy home. Sighing, the general took the boots handed to him by Meagan. He reached inside one and felt something lodged in the toe. Tugging, he pulled out a red headband. Dropping the boot, Alexanee pulled open the cloth.

"It seems we have found the hunting band, Great Mother," said Alexanee.

"Is it what you are searching for?" asked Meagan.

Alexanee ordered, "Hand me that bowl."

Meagan meekly handed Alexanee a washing bowl filled with clean water. Alexanee gingerly put the filthy cloth into the water and swished it around several times. Squeezing the water out, Alexanee examined the headband under a lamp. The cloth was a dull red with no markings on it as Timon had worn that day.

"This looks like it could be the scribe's hunting band. With your permission, Great Mother, I would like to take this and study it."

"Of course, General Alexanee. I realize how this accident may hang heavily on your shoulders, but you are not at fault. Take what you need."

Alexanee bit his tongue in order not to respond to the implication he was somehow to blame for the hunting accident. "I worry about the safety of the empress always, as do all of her most loyal subjects."

Maura patted Meagan's sleeve. "I'm in good hands now. There is no need to worry."

Alexanee bristled at the implied insult. He felt the blood rush to his hawk-like face. "Just one more thing, Great Mother."

"Yes."

"We could not find your amulet." He watched Maura's face.

Remaining stoic, Maura replied, "That is because I was not wearing it that day."

"I see. I say this only because you have worn it every day since Atetelco."

"You will see it again."

"I just wanted to make sure I had not overlooked anything."

"The amulet is safe and in my keeping. Thank you, General Alexanee."

Bowing very low to hide his distress, Alexanee backed out.

With the general safely gone, the High Priestess emerged from the shadows. "Do you think he suspects?"

Maura threw her covers off. "Yes. Alexanee is a shrewd man, but he can't prove anything for now. He will bide his time." Maura turned toward the High Priestess. "And I will bide mine."

14

Jezra studied maps.

They were placed on the table with great care. Her pale hair hung down, clinging to her graceful shoulders. Her forehead furrowed as she poured over the current location of Maura. "Why is she moving so slowly?" complained Jezra.

"Perhaps to cause you to be impatient and make a mistake," answered Mikkotto, looking like a well-pampered lizard lounging on a couch covered with costly material. A servant massaged Mikkotto's strong hands as the baroness stared at the elaborately painted ceiling depicting strange mythological creatures.

"She could have been here months ago, and this would have been over. I hate this waiting."

Mikkotto sighed. She disliked the young aganess who possessed no finesse for either politics or war. She thought Jezra stupid. No, stupid wasn't the right word to use; imperceptive was a better choice. "Meanwhile, you solidify your position in power here more each day, and the warehouses are being stocked with grain. You can withstand a siege indefinitely."

Jezra pushed her hair behind her ears. "I think we should venture out and engage her."

Mikkotto closed her eyes and sank deeper into the couch. "I think we should stay right where we are."

"I can't stand this waiting."

"My dear, you will find that most of life is spent waiting," replied Mikkotto, shifting her position so the servant could massage her other hand. "It would be better not to get into a huff about something you cannot change."

"What can't I change?"

"You cannot change Maura's progress. She has her own agenda. You can only watch, observe, formulate, and prepare to take action when finally needed." Mikkotto sighed under her breath. She thought this woman was truly tiresome since everything needed to be explained. "I have tried to kill her twice, and each time she has escaped. Maura was either born under a very lucky star, or she is a very capable person." Mikkotto lowered her eyelids.

Jezra seemed unimpressed. "Perhaps you are not as

great a warrior as you claim. We might try different methods this time."

Mikkotto did not rise to the bait as much as she wanted to backhand the insulting wench standing before her. She had thought Anqarians to be sophisticated and knowledgeable, but this person was a mere trifle, an annoyance at best.

Under heavy lids, she watched Jezra turn back to her maps and study them again. Indeed, Jezra was a beauty. Mikkotto could easily see how a very young Dorak would have been infatuated with Jezra's pale hair, cornflower blue eyes, and pouty lips. Still, even after having Dorak's child, Jezra's figure was ripe and luscious with wide hips that accentuated her small waist, and full breasts, which swayed invitingly when she walked.

"How old were you when you married Dorak?" asked Mikkotto impulsively.

Jezra looked up from her maps. "Sixteen. He was seventeen."

"How old are you now?"

"How old are you?" snapped back Jezra.

Mikkotto smiled slowly. "I am forty-eight."

Jezra appraised Mikkotto's muscular body. The Hasan Daegian was a tall, powerfully built woman with long black hair. Her face possessed intelligent, dark eyes that darted beneath arched brows, like a predator hunting its next meal. Full, sensuous lips softened the sharp angles of Mikkotto's cheekbones.

If Mikkotto's face had belonged to a man, Jezra would have been more at ease with it. It was odd to see such blatant ambition and arrogance in a woman. Jezra thought back to her people. She had seen such a countenance on the faces of women from the House of Magi, who walked about the city in long blue-green robes. They had been respected and honored among the Anqarians. There were no such women among the Bhuttanians. *I have lived among the Bhuttanians too long*, thought Jezra. *I have forgotten the power of women.*

"I am twenty-six this year," confided Jezra.

"Ah," cooed Mikkotto, disappointed Jezra had not commented on her youthful appearance.

Interested in telling her story, Jezra was glad for a chance to talk to someone, even a Hasan Daegian. "My father owned the largest banking house in Anqara. It was he who serviced the Aga of Bhuttan with loans used to underwrite the expansion of Zoar's power. My father would meet Zoar secretly at the border of Anqara and Bhuttan, because he was afraid of what the other Anqarians would do if they knew he conducted business with Zoar."

Mikkotto inspected her hands after the servant had

finished massaging them. She rolled on her stomach and bade the servant to rub her feet through the soles of her slippers.

Hatred welled up in the servant's eyes but died as soon as Mikkotto glanced in her direction.

Jezra witnessed the servant's momentary indiscretion, but did not rebuke. She could hardly scold a servant for feeling the same way she did. "You are not paying attention to me," chided Jezra. She was not used to being ignored.

"I have listened to every syllable you have uttered," answered Mikkotto, trying to hide a yawn. "I want to know how you became Dorak's wife."

Jezra was pleased Mikkotto had asked her to continue. "It wasn't long before Zoar owed my father a vast fortune. The expansion had not yielded the fortune Zoar thought he was going to make. My father, seeing opportunity, agreed to forgo part of the debt."

"You were to marry Dorak and become part of the royal family," Mikkotto interjected.

"Yes, that is correct," retorted Jezra, looking a little miffed Mikkotto had stolen her thunder.

"So old Zoar kept his word," expressed Mikkotto, thinking of her former lover.

"In a manner of speaking."

Mikkotto lifted her head from the couch. "I am

waiting," urged the Baroness.

"I was promised to Dorak as a child and returned to Anqara to live with my father. Coming of age, I was reunited with Dorak and expected to act as his wife and he my husband." Jezra paused as if reliving painful memories.

"But you were not made princess royal."

Jezra shook her head as though unable to speak. She finally dropped into a chair next to Mikkotto. She had a defeated look about her.

"This is a very old story. I can finish it for you." Mikkotto rolled over and placed her arms behind her head. "Time passed. You had a baby. Dorak lost interest in you, and because you were not made princess royal, he could afford to ignore you. You pleaded. You begged. You threatened. The more you shouted, the less he paid attention to you until he paid no attention at all. In fact, you had become an embarrassment to him, a little nobody without money and power."

"Sounds about right," Jezra affirmed bitterly, while watching a slave light the oil lamps.

"And then he met Maura, and you realized you had lost him for good." Mikkotto licked her lips. She liked inflicting pain, especially on someone like Jezra, who displayed every emotion on her pretty but uninteresting face. Mikkotto compared it to watching clouds casting a dark shadow across a sunny meadow filled with flowers. The baroness knew she shouldn't give the aganess any cause to dislike her, but Jezra was such an easy target, Mikkotto found it hard to resist attacking.

"I hate her. She took my place. She must hate me, too."

"I doubt Maura feels anything about you one way or the other."

"What do you mean by that?"

Mikkotto shrugged. "I doubt Maura could even describe to someone what you look like. This is not a personal contest with her. She is coming to secure the crown for her daughter and to ensure that Bhuttan never regains superior military strength over Hasan Daeg."

"That's absurd! She knows the army has been split in two, dividing the Empire. Maura could have easily kept the Bhuttanians in her camp loyal to her banner and slept easily at night knowing that we are coping with a civil war within the walls of the city. We have neither the time nor resources to traipse back across this continent to reconquer Hasan Daeg."

"What you say is correct for now, but sooner or later, someone would win and then begin rebuilding the army. Without conquered land, Bhuttan cannot exist. All of her resources have been exhausted. Bhuttan would have to expand its territory down the road. It may take twenty years, maybe forty, but Bhuttanians would again one day stand at the borders of Hasan Daeg."

Mikkotto was many things, most of them unpleasant, but Jezra had to admit the older woman was a cunning tactician. The aganess saw possible uses for Mikkotto, other than being a nuisance who abused the slaves in her palace. She realized that Zoar had seen this, too, in Mikkotto and had taken her for his mistress for reasons other than pleasure.

Taking no notice of the aganess' scrutiny, Mikkotto continued, "You, however, fight Maura for personal reasons. That is why you will make mistakes."

Jezra huffed, "You make her sound like an old soul who has walked the wheel many times. Maura is younger than me!"

"She has mated with the Bogazkoy."

"That stupid tree is nothing but an old wives' tale. Zoar looked for it for almost two decades without finding a shred of evidence to support its existence. We have spies telling us everything that goes on in Maura's camp, and in two years, not one of them has seen or heard anyone talking about this Bogazkoy."

"It does exist."

"Have you seen it? Has someone brought you a

piece of its bark or made a tea from its leaves? I tell you it is a lie!"

"How do you explain Maura's blue skin?" asked Mikkotto angrily, feeling that her honor was questioned.

"The blue skin is created by vegetable dye she puts on herself. If you like, I can be green tomorrow and purple the next."

Mikkotto snorted at the suggestion.

Jezra laughed. "I can't believe you accept those tales as truth. It's mumbo-jumbo. Now, this is real power." Jezra extended her hand and pointed a finger at Mikkotto. A slender bolt of blue light surged from her index finger and flashed toward Mikkotto, who barely dodged it.

Jezra giggled while inspecting her finger. She found it bruised and dark. Sucking on it for a few seconds, she rubbed her finger on her dress.

Mikkotto inspected the hole the blue light had made in the couch. A small swirl of smoke drifted from the burnt opening. She smelled the cushion and placed her finger in the hole. Regarding Jezra, she sneered, "Well, aren't you full of surprises?"

Smug, Jezra replied, "I have my moments."

"I'm just wondering where a nice little girl like you learned something like that?"

"I had to do something to fill in the time with

Dorak gone so much."

Mikkotto threw the cushion out the window. She paused for a moment and then walked around the couch, standing before Jezra. Taking Jezra's chin in her hand, Mikkotto squeezed until she was hurting the self-proclaimed aganess.

Jezra gasped from Mikkotto's tight grip. She thought it audacious that the Hasan Daegian woman dared to touch her. Bringing her hand up, she pointed at Mikkotto, but the stronger woman grabbed her hand, pointing it at the ceiling. A weak beam emerged from Jezra's finger only to sputter and die. Mikkotto cautiously turned Jezra's hand toward her so that she could inspect more closely. Patting down the aganess arm, Mikkotto tore open Jezra's sleeve so she could feel the younger woman's armpit, rib cage, and chest.

"No apparatus," muttered Mikkotto, talking to herself. "You feel normal."

"Let go of me!" Jezra commanded through her teeth.

Putting on a sly smile, Mikkotto gave Jezra a shove while releasing her.

Rubbing her wrist, Jezra spat, "How dare you touch me!"

Mikkotto plopped down on the damaged couch and crossed her legs. "You've got yourself a little talent there, Aganess. What else can you do?"

"Are you mocking me?"

"On the contrary, I am quite interested. I would like to know what else you can do."

"That is my secret."

Mikkotto shook her head. "I'm sorry, my dear, but it is our secret. You see, I didn't travel all this way to be put off by a mere banker's daughter. You will tell me your secrets, or I will show you my talent. It is unique, but quite unforgiving when applied. I have a gift for inflicting pain."

Cracking her knuckles, Mikkotto gave Jezra a smile that sent tremors down the young woman's back.

"Do you wish to see what I can do?" Mikkotto continued with silky menace.

"I can have you executed for threatening me."

Mikkotto laughed, showing her white, straight teeth. "Your people won't execute me. I was Zoar's mistress and his intended empress. They would never harm me to protect you. It's just not their way." The baroness stretched. "Too bad he died so unexpectedly, but I guess that was good news for you. One step closer to the throne, or so you thought. That was before Dorak married Maura. Now everything is askew."

"What do you want of me? Why are you here?"

"No need to get hostile. I don't want your throne. I

hate Bhuttan and everyone in it. These people are barbarians." Looking as though she wanted to spit on the floor, Mikkotto refrained. "I want Hasan Daeg. All of her. Give me Hasan Daeg, and I will help you to the throne of Bhuttan."

Jezra felt overwhelmed by Mikkotto's indomitable will and force of character, but she was shrewd enough to realize the Hasan Daegian could be of immense value to her. "You will have Hasan Daeg as long as you open the borders to free commerce, and you ship me a thousand wagons of grain each harvest."

"We could have a crop failure."

"That's your problem."

Mikkotto mulled over the idea, but Jezra knew the baroness was bluffing. Jezra could not show she was intimidated by the older woman. "Take it or leave it," she barked.

Clapping her hands together in triumph, Mikkotto sprang off the couch and extended her hand to Jezra.

Jezra clasped Mikkotto's forearm in agreement.

"There is one more thing."

Jezra wearily sighed. "What is it?"

"I want the head of Maura brought to me."

Jezra returned a cheeky smile to Mikkotto. "I thought you said this was not personal."

"I lied."

"Of course, I would never think of interfering with a guest's pleasure. It would not be considered hospitable."

The baroness, dressed in solemn black, lowered her head and kissed Jezra's hand. "To the Aganess of Bhuttan."

Jezra inclined her head in reply to Mikkotto's kiss. "To the Queen of Hasan Daeg."

Mikkotto looked at Jezra. "To the death of Maura!"

Jezra smiled. "To anyone's death who stands in our way."

Mikkotto understood Jezra's sly meaning and wondered how long before she had to kill Jezra. She hoped it wouldn't be long.

15

Timon stood in a little cluster.

He tried to blend in the crowd of arguing merchants, mingo drivers, soldiers of fortune, and the general ragtag of men and women who followed wherever mayhem and tragedy existed, seeking their luck.

The guards, who manned the western gate, looked tired and forlorn as they gazed over the clamoring knot of humanity pressing their claims to enter the city of Bhuttani. The guards carefully considered every person's papers while searching cargo for contraband that might be sold on the black market. The only time the guards' faces relaxed a tiny bit was when they dealt with a Sivan, who always waited patiently with hands folded into a neat bouquet upon his belly.

Noticing how the guards were easygoing with any Sivan, Timon moved his position behind some mercenaries and stood near a small group of Sivans. He turned to tell KiKu to follow him, but the master spy and his women were behind Timon, standing mute with their hands folded, imitating the Sivan merchants.

Timon smiled at KiKu. He should have known that the sharp eyes of KiKu would have missed nothing.

KiKu's face remained expressionless.

"You there!" commanded a guard, poking Timon in the shoulder. "What do you want?"

Timon's head snapped around, catching sight of a huge Bhuttanian looming over him. This soldier was even large by Bhuttanian standards. Timon felt his throat constrict involuntarily.

"I am Timon de Berechiah from the Qued Zem province," stated Timon, surprised that his voice sounded steady. "I have come to seek entrance as a novice to the temple of Bhuttu." He handed the guard his papers.

"That's all we need, another religious fanatic," harrumphed the guard. He read the papers and then squinted at Timon. "Who are they?" he queried, thumbing at KiKu and the women.

"My servants," replied Timon calmly, even though his heart pounded.

The swarthy giant of a guard strode over to KiKu, who did not flinch as the Bhuttanian breathed on his head. Instead, KiKu looked up and confronted the guard with his hypnotic eyes.

The guard gasped slightly and stepped back a little from KiKu. "By the beards of the gods, he is a Bilboa."

"Yes," said Timon, stepping closer to distract the tall fellow. "I got him in Salamanca."

"I've only seen a few. Their eyes always give me the jitters," stated the guard, referring to KiKu's glowing red eyes with several black squares for twin pupils in each eye.

Timon felt the sweat break out on the back of his neck. He replied, "That's why they are so valuable. They can see just as well in the night as in the day."

The guard turned and spat on the ground. "Exactly. This man should be working as a scout for the army. He is too valuable to be working as a mere servant. I am going to confiscate him."

Timon moved to intercept the guard. "If you would check his papers, you will find he has been released from all military duty as he is physically unfit. He is damaged in the head."

The guard grunted and motioned to KiKu to re-move his turban.

KiKu remained impassive.

Timon quickly intervened again. "They will respond to only one master. Allow me," said Timon stepping between the guard and KiKu. "Take off your turban and allow this man to touch you."

The Bilboa dutifully took off his turban, causing dark red locks to fall on his shoulders. He bowed his head toward the soldier.

The guard took out his dagger.

Timon became alarmed.

The guard, seeing Timon's dismay, said, "He could have lice," and went through the Bilboa's head, tapping with the blunt side of the dagger until he found a metal plate on the right side of the servant's head. He tapped it harder until it gave a little ring.

KiKu popped his head up, looking a little worse for wear.

Grumbling, the guard affixed a wax seal on Timon's papers.

Timon grunted his thanks and started to move through the gate.

"Young one," called out the guard. "You'd be better to go to a whore house. You'll not be happy at the temple. Strange things are going on there. Beware!"

As Timon thought to question the guard, KiKu gave him a push forward. "Better not test your luck or my head again," he hissed through his teeth.

Timon marched through the spiked gate with his servants following obediently behind him. He was stopped again on the other side of the massive wall but with little fanfare this time. Another guard looked at the wax seal, still warm, and pressed a wooden stamp on it. He grunted, and Timon went anxiously on his way into the vast city of Bhuttani, capital of Bhuttan.

While a Sivan caravan blocked his way to the main thoroughfare, Timon took time to study the buildings leading out into the main part of the city from the western side. The buildings were constructed of sandstone with immense wooden beams acting as supports. Solidly built, each building—many having as many as five stories—served as a mini fortress. Some were obviously private homes with laundry hanging from the upper windows, safe from dust stirred up by the myriad of feet and hooves below. Each home was the same with the first floor used as a stable and the second floor as a storage facility with rooms for servants. The upper floors were for the owner and his family where dust, odors, and bugs would be less of a problem.

Timon was bowled over by the putrid stench in the street. Holding his travel shawl up so that he could cover his mouth and nose, he quickly observed what was creating such a horrible stench. On either side of the dirt-packed street, he saw a ditch had been dug to accommodate each house's dirty water, food scraps, and body waste.

Timon remembered crying as a boy being carried through the wretched streets of Bhuttani by his pale, solemn father to meet the aga. He remembered pinching his nose and begging to be taken home because "everything stinks here." Timon shook the unpleasant memory from his head.

A small group of Sivans passed Timon's little entourage. with their elaborate headdresses covering their entire faces except for their eyes. Timon strongly suspected that all of the Sivans had herbs wrapped in the cloth near their noses to protect them from the smell and illness caused by the refuse in the streets. Timon wished he had the foresight to wear a similar costume.

Only KiKu seemed unaffected by the foulness. He stood patiently as only a Bilboa could, waiting for his master to command him. Even a swarm of biting flies passing through the street did not cause KiKu to move a muscle.

After slapping the obnoxious flies away from his eyes and nose, Timon exclaimed, "This is awful! We must find an inn." Timon hurriedly marched down the street, pushing his way through the throng of people, and occasionally asking where a respectable inn might be found. Most ignored him, but a kind man stopped and gave Timon the name of a good inn and directions.

Timon profusely thanked him as the man briskly went on his way. No one liked to tarry outside for long if they could possibly avoid it.

As Timon swiftly negotiated the streets of Bhuttani, he was reminded again of his entry into the city as a child and his final emergence ten years later as a young man, marching with the aga's army, hoping someday to escape to his home. He had not seen his mother those ten years; the only contact with her were letters written full of love and longing. He doubted he would know her if he spied her on the street. Timon vowed if he survived this mission, he was going home to see his mother, and nothing would be able to stop him.

Deep in thought, Timon motioned KiKu to move to the head of their little group so the inn would be found more quickly, since the streets were not marked. After many twists and turns, KiKu found the inn, and waited outside with the exhausted women until Timon returned after making arrangements with the corpulent innkeeper.

They were shown two adjoining rooms on the second floor. There was only one bed and no chairs. When Timon complained, the innkeeper shrugged and said nothing else was available.

"Take it or not," the innkeeper snarled in a squeaky voice. "It's all we have."

Seeing the innkeeper was telling the truth, Timon threw him a gold coin. The innkeeper caught the coin with his apron and left the room with a happy smile on his whiskered face.

Pearl opened the shutters of a little window, which offered the only ventilation in the room, and peered out. "It could be worse," she said. "We could be stuck on the first floor with the animals."

The twins groaned while throwing their belongings on a dirty rug that covered the floor of their room.

There was a knock on the door. A maidservant entered with an arm full of reeds. Looking around for a good spot, she threw them on the floor, and then covered them with clean coverlets. Since the women lodgers appeared to be menials like herself, the maidservant did not curtsy as she left the room.

Pearl took a vial from her little satchel and turned back the coverlets on all of the pallets and the only bed in Timon's room, sprinkling a liberal amount of green liquid on them until everyone complained about the acrid smell. "Well, now you won't have to worry about bed bugs," she muttered defensively.

Exhausted from the journey, Timon spread out on the bed, ready to take a long nap. A shadow passed over his face, causing Timon to wearily open his burning eyes.

KiKu stood over him with a disgruntled look on his face. "I hope you are not thinking of resting now that we have entered the city."

"It will be dark in several hours," answered Timon. "It is too late to go to the temple."

"That is correct, but you will need to get ready for tomorrow. You will need to have your clothes washed. A bath for us is in order. If we don't tell the innkeeper now, the hot water will be used up. Someone will need to provide food and drink."

Timon flung himself from the bed. "All right, all right. I will take care of these matters." He opened a pouch full of coins. "You see about the water, and I will procure food. The women can wash my clothes. Uhm . . ." Timon stopped short as KiKu violently shook his head.

"My wives are tired and have suffered much on this journey. They need all the rest they can."

Timon nodded in agreement. They were so good at acting he sometimes forgot they were not servants. "You pay for the water, and I will go out into the city and get food. I will be less likely to be recognized, even though you do look like a Bilboa. There is no reason to take any chances."

KiKu bowed very low and salaamed, pressing his palm to his forehead. "Your will, my lord."

"My will, my arse!" complained Timon as he stomped out of the cramped room and down the dusty steps to the street door, holding onto a leather pouch. A doorman opened the entrance for him after Timon asked questions about where to purchase fruit and fried bread. The doorman told Timon the inn was serving roasted borax that was only a day old. Timon drooled at the thought of meat, but ventured out into the city anyway because the twins ate only vegetables or fruit. He would buy some meat for himself though, he thought happily. And off he went.

16

Timon returned.

He lugged a pouch stuffed with ripe fruit, followed by a slapdash of a boy whose arms were loaded with cheeses and several types of bread. As there was no table, the boy merely dropped his load on the floor and waited patiently for his promised reward.

Hearing commotion stemming from Timon's room, the women knocked and rushed in. Seeing the food on the floor, they cried out with both pleasure at the sight of it and disgust that it was lying on the dirty floor. They laid a clean shawl flat on the floor and arranged the food into an appealing display.

The young boy tried to help the women, but they pushed him away, crying that he was too dirty.

Pearl gave the boy some fruit and told him to stand by the door.

The boy smiled at Pearl wondering at her kindness.

Timon gave him a large hunk of bread and a small copper coin. The boy's eyes lit up as he shoved the bread in his mouth while running out of the room. He feared the young man might change his mind and ask for the coin and food back.

Timon sat on his bed and KiKu on his pallet as they watched the women fuss with the meal.

In addition to arranging for hot water, KiKu also garnered several skins of wine, which the women placed along with the bread.

Timon noticed the women's hair was wet so he assumed that they had already washed off the fetor of the road. They smelled fresh. Hittals were like Hasan Daegians—they loved to take baths.

The women clicked along at a furious pace in their language. Timon liked hearing their happy chatter. Glancing at KiKu, Timon assumed he liked to hear it, too, as KiKu's facial expression relaxed watching his wives prepare their supper.

Finally, the women waved the men over to the colorful shawl. In true harem fashion of Hittal, the women massaged the feet and shoulders of the men as they ate and drank wine. And in true male fashion of Hittal, KiKu and Timon ate quickly and retired to their beds so the women could eat.

The women took a leisurely dinner that included eating, laughing, and talking while occasionally stealing glances at the men who seemed to have fallen asleep. Before retiring to their rooms, they wrapped the remaining food in clean cloths and stored them in leather bags, which were kept at the foot of Timon's bed. They then dragged in a wooden tub filled with water and a pitcher from their room. After making sure everything was in its place, they went to their own compartment and shut the door.

As soon as their door closed, Timon sat straight up and, leaning over the side of the bed, rummaged through the leather bags tearing off a hunk of bread and cheese.

"Throw me some, too," said KiKu, also sitting up.

Timon learned that caring Hittal husbands did not make their hungry wives wait long for their meals. They would eat enough to satisfy the women, but not enough to satisfy their stomachs. After the women retired, KiKu was always sneaking off in the dark to eat more, as were Hittal husbands the world over.

"Why don't you and your wives dine together?" Timon asked.

KiKu seemed appalled at his question. "The man is head of Hittal family. It is disrespectful not to serve him first."

"Then why don't we just have dinner instead of sneaking off into all hours of the night trying to get something to eat?"

"It is unkind to make women and children wait to eat when they are hungry."

Timon tried again. "Why don't we put food in our pockets to eat later?"

"The women would see and be upset if they thought we were not eating until we are full. It would cast dishonor upon them."

Timon finally understood the Hittal logic. "And it would cast dishonor upon a man if he ate while a woman stood by hungry."

KiKu nodded enthusiastically. "Men eat until the edge of hunger is taken off and then let women and children eat till they are full. Men eat later, but mustn't let women see, or they will be dishonored. Everyone knows everything, but if you don't see, you are not dishonored. All Hittal men wait. It makes little sense anymore, but no one knows how to end it without casting aspersions, so we cope." KiKu flashed a big grin. "It is a small thing for me to wait."

Timon smiled back.

KiKu was right. It was not a burden. At times, he even liked to play the game, but tonight, he was ravenous and stuffed cheese into his mouth while reaching for the wineskin.

After eating his portion, Timon lay in his bed, patting his belly. He hesitated for a moment, looking at the tub, only to turn over after deciding that he would bathe in cold water tomorrow morning. Before he could delve into a deep sleep, he felt tapping on his foot. Timon opened one eye.

"What are you doing?"

"I am going to sleep," replied Timon, wondering what KiKu wanted now. He was beginning to annoy Timon.

"We must go soon."

"Go where?"

"To rendezvous with our contact. Usually, I would go alone, but if I die, you must know how to reach the temple contact."

"Can't this wait until morning?" pleaded Timon, eyeing his pillow.

Exasperated with Timon, KiKu huffed, "NO!" He thought the boy lazy at times. "We must meet tonight before you go to the temple in the morning."

Timon knew better than to argue with KiKu. "Wake me up when it is time." He turned over.

KiKu hit his foot again. Timon raised his head a little. "You have not washed your clothes or your body yet. It must be done now."

"Can't you do it?"

KiKu sat on his pallet. "Not my clothes, not my body."

Timon jumped off the bed in a foul mood. "Now I know why you took the disguise of a Bilboa. They never bathe."

KiKu never heard the scribe as he was fast asleep on his pallet with his hand on the hilt of his dagger.

Resenting the fair ladies and KiKu for making him perform menial tasks, Timon grumbled and muttered as he washed the outfit he was going to wear to the temple. He also mended a little hole he found in the jacket. Afterwards, he gave himself a sponge bath and washed his hair. He braided his long, dark hair and tied it with a leather thong. He put on a dark pair of trousers and a dark shirt from his bags to wear for the night. Weary from his tasks, Timon fell asleep for what seemed only for a few minutes before he felt KiKu's strong hand on his shoulder giving him a tight squeeze.

"Time to go."

17

T imon opened his eyes.

A shaft of moonlight feebly entered the room, out-lining KiKu so that his eyes glowed like coals. The glowing red eyes in the darkness startled Timon, even though he knew they were a disguise.

KiKu moved silently across the floor and gracefully slid through the window, disappearing into the night.

Timon sighed and tried to cross the floor as quietly as KiKu. It seemed to him every floorboard squeaked. Remembering that a storage floor was underneath him and not other guests, Timon breathed easier. The young prince-turned-scribe-turned-spy pushed his frame through the narrow opening, getting several splinters from the wooden jambs. He silently cursed, but slid through and climbed down to the ground. He landed with a heavy thud. Looking around, he could not find KiKu.

A large hand reached out from a dark corner and pulled him in. KiKu clasped a hand over the mouth of a surprised Timon. "Shhh. Be quiet. You make more noise than a band of drunken freebooters. Remember your training."

Timon breathed deeply as he had been taught by KiKu and controlled his intake of air until his breathing was silent and steady. As trained, Timon stopped narrowly focusing on his surroundings and began to "see." He began with "splatter vision," which used his peripheral sight and focused his hearing. There was no one in the street. Timon's eyes shot up the surrounding buildings, studying the windows. Why would people get up in the middle of the night? Ask the important questions, KiKu always coached, then you will get the important answers. Timon thought, *A person would be up to get a drink of water, comfort a child, get fresh air, or relieve themselves.* No one appeared to be at a window getting air. He did not hear the squalls of any child. The street seemed deserted. Did his gut tell him the street was empty? Yes, it did.

KiKu, the true master of penetrating the unseen, slid out of the corner shadow and effortlessly glided door to door down the street, hiding in the dark recess of their entrances. Timon followed suit, but was sure he was making noise while KiKu seemed like a specter drifting on moonbeams. Every so often, KiKu would stop and take in his surroundings. If he felt nothing was askew, they continued.

After what seemed a long time, Timon's thighs burned from squatting in doorways. They finally came to a street where people spilled out onto its cobbled pathway, talking loudly and acting rambunctiously. Timon had never been to this part of the city, but he recognized a pleasure district when he saw one.

KiKu stepped out into the street, weaving slightly as though he was mildly drunk.

Timon immediately assumed the role of a companion assisting his sodden friend to negotiate the winding street. Light splashed out of the taverns' doorways, which helped Timon step over drunken soldiers asleep in the middle of the street. From the upstairs floors, women's laughter that sounded both lascivious and empty drifted down like a soft breeze. They could hear the not-so-quiet murmurs of men and women talking in deep husky tones and sometimes the slapping, wet noises made by frantic lovemaking. Boys, with painted faces and wearing handsome gowns, called out to him from windows.

Timon hoped the light coming from the taverns and doorways was weak enough to hide his shamed face. He was embarrassed to be in such a place, even though he was on a mission. No person of any character would hire a companion for such purposes. Only the meanest of spirit and the poorest in society would willingly expose themselves to lovemaking such as this. At least that was the way in his world. His mother had been very firm about that.

Halfway down the street, a curvaceous woman wrapped in a heavy shawl and veil approached them. "You there, would you like a tumble?"

Irritated with her presence, Timon was about to send her away when KiKu brusquely pushed the woman back against a wall. He lowered his pants as the woman wrapped her legs around his waist. KiKu jerked his head toward Timon, "Kiss her, you fool. A patrol is coming!"

Timon hurried over to the thrusting couple doubly embarrassed by the grunts KiKu was making. The woman cupped her arms around Timon. "Kiss me." Seeing Timon's reluctance, she added, "Act as though you are kissing me."

Timon bent his head toward the woman and could smell expensive perfumes on the woman's hair and skin. The scent was intoxicating. Without thinking, he touched her skin with his lips and then covered her mouth. Much to his surprise, she kissed back. Much to his surprise again, he kissed harder. He opened his eyes and saw the woman had open hers as well, but her eyes were searching the street behind him.

Timon heard the patrol marching and closed his eyes. His heart pounded from fear, and his knees felt weak. He kissed the woman harder.

An iron hand with a spiked knuckle band gripped Timon's shoulder and swung him around. Timon's eyelids snapped open to reveal a grizzled Bhuttanian combat soldier with a bulbous nose, who seemed very disturbed that he was on patrol so early in the morning or so late at night, considering his viewpoint. The soldier's one good eye swept over Timon. He called to his companions, "He's not one of us." The soldier pushed Timon out of the way as he tried to pry KiKu from the woman, who was making all sorts of gasps and grunts.

KiKu pulled out a short knife with one hand as he held onto the woman with the other. He jabbed near the soldier's gut. "Can't you see I'm busy!"

For a moment, the soldier seemed stunned and then grinned, slapping Timon on the chest. "A man after my own heart," he said laughing. "A man should be able to fight and screw at the same time. Take note from your comrade, young friend."

Timon nodded weakly and resumed kissing the panting woman. The soldier rejoined his patrol, as they heaved passed-out drunken soldiers into a large cart, dragging them back to their quarters where they would be sobered up and sent back to their tasks.

KiKu made a strangled cry as though he had climaxed and lowered the woman's legs to the ground. "Take my place," said KiKu pulling up his pants.

Timon looked at him horrified. "I can't. My tribe is very strict about these things."

The spylord's face grew angry, and he thrust his hands out toward the younger man in such a menacing way that the woman quickly pulled Timon to her and began untying his trousers. "It's just play acting," she whispered into his ears. "Hold me up to give me support," she said as she wrapped her legs around Timon's bare middle. Timon was relieved to feel cloth between him and the strange woman. Slowly, Timon began moving between the woman's legs as KiKu kissed and fondled her.

"Master, you have come at an auspicious time," she whispered between tiny cries of faked pleasure. "The sightings are occurring more frequently and with greater clarity."

"When was the last sighting?" KiKu whispered under his audible grunts and curses.

"Night before last. The priest came to me, his mind much disturbed. He had seen a strange beast—a human covered with feathers like a bird and possessing giant wings. The creature knelt before the priest and begged for release. Then the vision disappeared like a puff of smoke."

"Where had he seen this vision?"

"When he was lighting the oil lamps in the main sanctuary for midnight prayers. He felt something brush his head and looked up. Right over him was the creature kneeling upside down. It gave Onxor quite a fright."

"Did he try to communicate with the Dini?"

The woman shook her head. "He was too alarmed."

"Then how does he know the creature begged for release?" asked Timon, puffing away.

"Because the creature was on his knees with his hands in supplication," explained the woman as though Timon was a simpleton. "The creature's mouth moved very slowly. Onxor could make out what he was saying."

"Is that all?" asked KiKu.

The woman nodded.

"Finish up," he said to Timon. "We need to go. It will soon be daybreak."

Timon copied KiKu's motions and let out a strangled cry. He smiled. "I thought that was rather good," he said of his performance. He let the woman's legs down gently and tossed her a few coins.

"You might even enjoy the real thing one of these

days," teased the woman.

No longer embarrassed, Timon looked at the woman's eyes peering at him over her veil. She had the most beautiful green eyes he had ever seen. He stared at them with the strong sensation he was falling.

KiKu nudged him. "Let's go."

"I'll follow you," answered Timon, unable to tear his eyes from the woman's face.

KiKu pushed Timon into the middle of the street only to have Timon swirl around and throw the woman a kiss.

She was nowhere to be seen.

Disappointed, Timon followed KiKu glumly back to the inn. As it would soon be daybreak, bakers, wine merchants, and beggars were already getting ready for the day's business. KiKu and Timon did not attempt to conceal their journey back to the inn.

Exhausted, Timon fell asleep the moment he touched his bed and snored loudly as KiKu lay awake on his pallet of straw. His eyes moved restlessly, panning the walls as he planned the release of the Dinii.

Even though Maura was fond of him, KiKu had no doubt she would carry out her threat to kill his family if he failed.

The Dinii must be released from the temple of Bhuttu!

18

Alexanee watched.

The Hasan Daegian women practiced the military moves he had taught them with their ponies. For the past several years, he had come to appreciate the agility of the small ponies and wondered how he could use them to their best advantage.

The main problem was that the rider was easy prey to enemy foot soldiers. She lacked the advantage of sitting high out of harm's way as one did on a Bhuttanian warhorse.

Still, the horses had their uses. He had been thinking about using the horses as a quick way to transport soldiers to a certain area in a battle where they would dismount to fight on foot. The horses would be trained to a series of whistles to return behind the battle lines. Alexanee was wiping the grime from his brow when he sensed a presence behind. He swung around, his hand on the hilt of his sword.

"Good afternoon, Lord Alexanee," Maura said.

Alexanee's eyes darted about the hillside.

Maura was alone except for her uultepes.

He bowed most graciously and clasped his fist to his chest.

Maura inclined her head.

Alexanee claimed, "I am afraid you startled me, Great Mother."

"How could I, a mere woman, startle the great general who conquered almost an entire continent?"

Alexanee's eyes narrowed. "Maura de Magela has never been a mere woman and will never be one. I did what I could for the service of my country."

Maura searched his dark, leathery face. Though still considered a young man by Hasan Daegian standards, Alexanee's face had deep creases that appeared like lines on a map. She could not find mockery in his dark eyes or the firm lines around his wide mouth. "I'll take that as a compliment, General Alexanee."

"As it was meant to be, Great Mother."

Maura smiled.

Alexanee was startled. He had never seen the empress give a genuine smile. It took him aback as she looked like a slip of a girl, innocent and pure, and not the feared despot she had become in recent years.

Maura's smile faded as she noticed his reaction. An expressionless face replaced the happy grin.

Alexanee regretted seeing her countenance change. This young woman should be worrying about what dress to wear and how many babies to have instead of whose head needed to be severed from his shoulders. His wife had given him a daughter, and he realized it wouldn't be long before his beautiful child would be Maura's age.

No woman should have been placed in a position of power so young, but Maura had been bred and trained to rule since the day she was born. She was not a normal young woman.

"Has the Great Mother come to watch the exercises?" he asked diplomatically. He hoped she would not bring up the hunting accident. It was nearly forgotten by all except for him. He had not been able to discover what Maura was planning, but he had not stopped trying to find out her secret.

"I want you to stop."

Alexanee's heart dropped. It was as he feared. She knew about his persistent inquiring about the scribe Timon. "I don't know to what you are referring, Great Mother," he bluffed.

Maura pursed her lips with impatience. "You have

good men around you—experienced, loyal, bright. It would be a pity if unfortunate things began happening to them." She looked at the Hasan Daegian women practicing on their ponies. "For example, falling off a horse and breaking their necks. Don't you agree that would be horrible, General Alexanee? Men, in the prime of their lives and so needed to fight in Bhuttani, dead and burned to ashes on the funeral pyre in this cold and barren land."

The general blinked against the strong light of the sun. Holding his hand up to shade his eyes, Alexanee realized he was getting a reprieve, and his men were being spared. "That would be most unfortunate," he agreed.

"Let's hope fate does not take such a turn."

"It will not," replied Alexanee, bowing. He felt gratitude toward her.

Maura turned back toward him. "One more thing, General Alexanee."

"Yes, Great Mother?"

"I have taken the liberty of sending for your wife and daughter. They should arrive this afternoon."

Alexanee stood speechless as though rooted to the ground.

"I can only guess how you must miss them. I thought we could both enjoy their company. After all,

Jezra might send an assassin to your home."

A pale Alexanee bowed. "I thank the Great Mother for her kindness."

"We wouldn't want to find either one of them with a dagger in their back, would we?"

"I will guard them with my life."

Maura smiled one of her "Empress" smiles. "That's what it may take. Come," she called to her uultepes.

They stood and swished their long tails at Alexanee as if to say, "See, there is more than one way to skin a general."

19

The Bilboa pounded harder.

He repeatedly banged on the grand metal doors guarding the entrance to the temple of Bhuttu, the war god of the Bhuttanians. He continued hammering until he thought his fists would turn into bloody hocks of meat. Defeated, he turned and slumped against the wall, shaking his head in defeat.

"There must be another way in," said Timon, disbelieving the priests would fail to answer their door even during a civil war.

"I know a way," a little voice piped.

Timon looked down.

Standing beside him like a lost borax calf was the young boy who had helped carry the provisions to the inn the other evening. Timon smiled at the scruffy urchin. "How is that, young man?"

The little boy puffed up his chest, trying to seem larger than he was. "If I show you, you must give me food and lodging for seven days." He peered eagerly up at Timon.

"I will give you enough coins for seven days," Timon agreed.

The little boy shook his head. "No. I don't want money. You must give me food and lodging for seven days," he replied firmly.

Puzzled, Timon turned to KiKu.

The spy was studying the young boy very carefully but said nothing.

The dirty scamp shrugged his shoulders. "You can pound here all day long, but no one will open the door. The doors have not opened since the civil war started."

"How do they get their supplies?" asked Timon, taking a very keen interest in the boy's knowledge.

The boy pointed to the walls. "They hoist everything they need over the walls."

Timon leaned his head near KiKu's ear. "There must be a door available if your contact got out last night."

"We cannot very well enter by the servant's door if you are applying as a novice," spat out KiKu, obviously irritated with the current situation. "We have to enter by the front. Since the front door is closed, it means they have ceased contact with the outside world, and they are not taking any more novices. This is a bad omen."

Timon asked, "How do the people worship Bhuttu if the temple is closed?"

The boy looked incredulously at Timon. "No one worships Bhuttu but by their death. He does not need live worshippers. He desires the sacrifice of life." The boy cocked his head at Timon. "Are you sure you are at the right temple?"

"That remains to be seen," muttered Timon, throwing out his hands in despair. Timon turned his back on the boy, staring at the mammoth doors. He had to get in, and he had to do it the proper way. He realized that if he entered by the servants' entrance, he would be chased off, therefore harming his chances of completing his mission. "What if we pose as merchants or servants, and then change our clothes once we get in?" he whispered to KiKu.

"We have already been spotted," KiKu answered. "I am sure someone from the temple is watching us even now and would guard against any possible intrusion. Also, that man sitting by the well could be a spy for any number of factions within the city. We must carry this out in our current disguises."

Timon knelt down as though he was trying to get a pebble out of his boot. He glanced surreptitiously at the well and did, indeed, see a man dressed as a peddler, flirting with servant women as they came to the well for water. He also watched the servant women, especially one who kept glancing in his direction. Timon concluded most of the women worked for businesses on the street, as most private homes had wells. Timon stood up and turned to KiKu. "I think there are two of them working together. The woman with the blue shawl seems very interested in us."

For a second, there was the note of satisfaction in KiKu's glaring red eyes. "Give the boy what he wants. We must get in."

Timon protested, "What if he gets in the way?"

"Then I will kill him."

Timon's mouth fell open and quickly closed. "If he serves us well, his life will be spared," Timon said firmly.

KiKu grunted.

Turning to the little boy, whose face was scrunched up trying to discern their whispers, Timon tousled his hair until he saw there were bugs. Not knowing what to do with his hand, Timon wiped his palm on his pants. "I will give you seven days lodging and food if you can open this door. However, I will sell you as a pleasure slave to the first soldier I see if you lie or steal from me."

The little boy nodded his head vigorously. "You do not need to worry, my lord. I will be very useful. I will be back. Stand there. Don't go away," he called as he ran off into the busy street. After a few minutes, the boy returned with a sharp rock and a stick. Kneeling by the temple doors, he dug a little rut in the dirt, going as far as he could underneath the thick metal. "I will need a gold coin," he said to Timon.

Reluctantly, KiKu handed the boy a coin.

The boy put the coin in the depression and, with his stick, pushed the coin farther and farther under the door. Pressing his ear on the metal, he waited.

KiKu also pressed his ear on the door and thought he heard scratching sounds from the other side.

The boy knelt and searched under the door. "I will need another coin."

KiKu kept giving him coins until five coins had disappeared under the metal doors.

Timon was about to give the boy a swift kick in his tiny backside when a side door, previously hidden to both KiKu and Timon, squeaked open just a tad.

A hoarse croaked, "What dost thou want?"

Peering at the shadow framing the doorway, Timon said, "My name is Timon de Berechial. I come from the province of Qued Zum. I have traveled a long way to apply for the priesthood in the service of Bhuttu."

Timon waited for a reply. There was silence from the doorway as Timon felt more than one pair of eyes studying him.

"Thou art a long way from home, brother," screeched a higher, younger voice from the doorway.

"Yeeesss," stammered Timon, losing his nerve. He felt KiKu's bony finger poke him in the back. "I have traveled for many months and endured many hardships. I come for nothing more than to serve Bhuttu and learn his ways."

"That is asking much from our Lord," replied the younger voice again. "What dost thou have to offer Bhuttu?"

"My mind, my body, my servants, and my wealth."

There was a long silence until the door slowly creaked opened. "Enter!" was the only response.

Timon, followed by KiKu and the boy, entered the dark doorway leading into the great temple of Bhuttu. Standing in a little alcove, they had to wait for their eyes to adjust to the darkness. Timon jumped a little when the door behind them slammed shut, causing all light to be extinguished. As KiKu stood behind him, Timon could not ask "his servant" if he could see anything, but he already knew what KiKu's answer would be.

The spy might be posing as a Bilboa, but that did not mean that KiKu had the same natural gifts as one, such as seeing in the dark. This thought caused Timon to stiffen his spine. Those watching would expect the turbaned Bilboa to see and act accordingly. "My servant might be able to see, but I assure you that I cannot nor will I command my servant to act if I cannot see where he is to step," said Timon into the darkness.

Utter silence answered Timon's words. He stood still and erect, trying to discern the tiniest movement. There was none. They waited until Timon gauged they had been standing almost three-quarters of an hour when an inner door opened.

A man, holding a lamp, stood barring its passageway. "Place thy weapons on the floor," he commanded.

Timon placed his dagger on the floor.

"Thy servant has one knife hidden in his turban and another stowed away in his boot."

Timon heard the clatter of metal fall to the stone floor followed by the unwrapping of cloth and then another clatter.

"May we now enter?" asked Timon, doing his best to sound authoritative.

"Thou mayest."

Timon strode through the door, glad to be out of the tiny little dungeon of a room. Bright sunlight struck like a hidden snake in the bush, causing Timon to shield his sensitive eyes with his hands. "Please wait a moment," he called to his guide walking on ahead. "My eyes must adjust. This light is blinding!"

"Thy servant might be able to guide thee," replied the man, retracing his steps to Timon's side.

"I would rather guide myself and not be led like a blind man," snapped Timon, holding his head down away from the glaring sun. "I refuse to go forward until I can see."

After several minutes, Timon opened his eyes tentatively and shielding them with a hand, glanced around. They were standing in the middle of a large courtyard. Hot air moved in waves across the paved walkway.

He blinked until his eyes adjusted to the almost white sunlight, though he could not stop squinting. "I've never seen such bright sunlight," he commented. He could see the outline of the man standing before him, but he could not make out the details of his face. Timon kept seeing black spots where the eyes should have been.

Turning, Timon saw his companions standing not too far from him. He tried to make eye contact with KiKu but immediately sensed trouble.

Because KiKu was supposed to be a Bilboa, KiKu had not lowered his head in the blinding sunlight, acting as though he could see, but Timon perceived KiKu's eyes were not making contact with anything. *He's blind!*

thought Timon. He snapped his attention back to the man standing before him. Starting to panic, Timon's mind went blank.

"I'm frightened," said the little boy to KiKu. "Hold my hand."

The boy placed his hand in the tall spylord's hand and tugged. "Master, may we go? This place frightens me."

"Be quiet!" barked Timon, acting as though he was irritated with the boy, but pleased the urchin had engineered an excuse to hold KiKu's hand and guide the tall spy out of the disturbingly bright sun. Sensing the boy understood their predicament and was trying to help, Timon said to their guide. "I am ready now."

The guide grunted in Bhuttanian fashion and led them across the courtyard to a magnificent building made of marble and alabaster. He knocked quietly on one of several doors. The door opened, and the guide bade them to enter.

They came into a long corridor. "Proceed to the end of the corridor," ordered the guide. "There you will find a door. Enter it."

The three adventurers did as they were told and found themselves in a lovely garden, which was lit by a more natural and subdued sunlight. Since no one appeared to greet them, Timon sat on a bench while the boy led KiKu to stand under a large tree where there was ample shade. Occasionally, KiKu would blink, indicating his sight was slowly coming back.

Timon lowered his head as though he was praying. Besides their guide, they had seen no one, though Timon could faintly hear chanting in the distance. He assumed they had arrived during morning devotionals. After what seemed an hour, Timon heard a door open and footfalls coming toward him. He did not stand, but continued with his praying. Out of the corner of his eye, he could see sandaled feet waiting patiently for him to finish. Making the sign on his chest of the eternal circle, which represented life, Timon rose to his feet, trying to look like a devoted servant of Bhuttu.

Before him stood a handsome middle-aged man dressed in a spotless yellow robe with only gold pendant earrings to adorn his person. The man was not dark like a Bhuttanian but fair like an Anqarian, though his hair was braided in Bhuttanian fashion.

Timon bowed very low. "My name is Timon de Berechiah. I come from Qued Zem. I am seeking entrance into the service of Bhuttu."

"My name is Onxor. One does not need to come here to order to serve Bhuttu. What else might thou want?"

"Your wisdom is great, my lord. I harbor the thirst

of ambition, which I thought might be quenched here."

"Rise, so I may see into thy eyes." The priest studied Timon for a long time. "Ambition in itself is not a fault, if tempered with logic and humility. Ambition can help a man ascend to great heights; however, ambition, without introspection, can be deadly for the man who harbors it and for the people around him as well." The priest peered over Timon's shoulder at KiKu and the young boy. "Thy servants are most unusual."

"The boy was not in my care until several hours ago. As he helped me gain entrance, I promised he would be in my keeping for seven days as reward for his services."

"Ah, he is most likely a street whelp." He turned away as though pained by the sight of the frail little boy. "Life in Bhuttani has been disrupted since the death of Aga Zoar. The people lack discipline in their duties. Orphans and beggars run amuck in the streets. The city is divided into factions that fight needlessly against each other, instead of uniting to fight the Deceiver, Maura." The priest lowered his excited voice. "But thou hast come to seek thy future, not to listen to a sermon about our society falling apart. Please follow me."

"Where are you taking me?"

"Thou art to stand before the judgment of the High Priest, Hilkiah."

Although Timon didn't like the sound of that, he

trailed the priest meekly out of the garden and through a maze of sumptuous corridors, until they came before two richly carved doors of rare black wood highlighted with gold relief. Timon glanced behind. KiKu and the boy followed at a respectful distance.

The priest tapped softly on the door. "I will take my leave now."

"Where are you going?" asked Timon, grabbing the priest's sleeve.

"Thou art to stand here until the door opens. That is all thee needs to do."

"How long will I be here?"

"As long as it takes the door to open. I must take my leave now. I hope I may see thy face again." Onxor turned and walked past KiKu and the boy, sharply turning the corner and then vanishing.

The boy tugged excitedly on KiKu's sleeve. "Did you see that? Did you see that? One moment he was there. The next disappeared. Just like that," said the boy, snapping his fingers.

KiKu scanned the hallway and studied the walls, saying nothing.

The boy wondered why he did not seem impressed.

KiKu signaled to Timon to turn around with a small motion of his finger. Frowning, Timon stood before the door awaiting entrance.

After several hours of waiting this time, Timon grew impatient. His legs were tiring, and he wanted to sit. His stomach growled. Angry that he was being made to wait so long, Timon tried one of the door handles and pushed. The door swung open just a little bit. Ignoring KiKu's warning cough behind him, Timon pushed the door open, stepping inside. Timon found himself in a beautiful, spacious garden filled with exotic flowers of bold colors. In the middle of the room meandered a bubbling stream spanned by a wooden bridge. A pale blue bird with yellow spots on its wings flew past Timon and landed on a strange tree, moving as though a wind was blowing its dark green-striped leaves. Timon wet his finger and held it up in the air. Just as he thought. There was no breeze.

Timon crossed the bridge, peering down into the stream. There were small colorful fish swimming between carefully placed reeds and ornamental water lilies. A tiny rock wren landed by Timon's hand on a rail, sounded a few peeps, and then dashed off. Timon could see that it flew into a stand of bamboo.

KiKu cautiously entered while the boy ran on ahead.

"Look at this!" exclaimed the boy, holding up a rock.

KiKu peered beneath the rock and held up several large gems worth a fortune in the outside world. He put them back and ordered the boy to replace the stone.

"Why don't we take them?" asked the boy. "They are doing nobody any good under a rock."

KiKu ignored the shrill plea of the boy.

"Why doesn't thee indeed?" a voice inquired.

Timon and KiKu swiveled around.

A man in a peasant tunic and trousers of coarse woven black cloth stood on a large boulder.

Timon had to remember to close his mouth for he had never seen another being that looked quite like the one standing above them. The man's skin was white as snow as was his close-cropped hair with his dark clothing serving only to create more of a contrast with his unusual skin tone, which Timon was sure the man intended. Timon found his voice. "Do we have the honor of addressing the High Priest, Hilkiah?" asked Timon, bowing very low.

KiKu and the boy followed suit.

"Thou dost. And the temple of Bhuttu has the honor of addressing Timon de Berechiah from Qued Zem. Welcome, fellow traveler. I hope thee hath enjoyed my private garden," he cooed, waving his hand.

Timon smiled. "It is most illuminating."

"In what way?"

"One may interpret this garden as the supreme garden, which we all hope to enter upon our deaths. Here is everything we are missing in our county. Fresh water, bountiful land that can grow a variety of plants, animals that can be harvested, and an aga's wealth in gems. Everything here is symbolic of our current deprivation; everything we need and desire."

The High Priest's face beamed with pleasure, mostly emanating from his shiny pinkish eyes. "That is exactly what I tried to accomplish with this garden; to make a model that would exemplify all that Bhuttan must have to be great. But let us not leave out beauty. I have tried to make it a place of wonder and color as well. As thou may knowest, many of our brethren have remained cold to aesthetics," he uttered, shrugging his shoulders a little. "But I have always been interested in pleasing sights." Hilkiah paused in speaking.

There was silence in the room, as Timon did not know how to respond at first. "If it pleases you, perhaps someday you might honor me with reciting the names and origins of these wondrous plants?" requested Timon, who thought this a most unusual interview.

"A servant of Bhuttu will guide thee to my office for a more personal conversation after thee hast rested. I see the whelp is in need of a bath."

The boy flinched at the mention of a bath, a most unusual custom for a Bhuttanian, but then priests were considered strange by the rest of the population.

"Rooms have been provided for thee and thy servants."

"I and my servants must humbly thank you for your hospitality," replied Timon, bowing again as did KiKu while pushing the boy's head down.

When they looked up, Hilkiah was gone.

Timon and KiKu did not seem surprised, but the boy could hardly contain his excitement. "They must be magicians or something!" he exclaimed. "They are better than the ones who perform in the market squares. I wish I could do that!"

"Hush!" commanded Timon, who was trying to organize his thoughts. He wanted to explore the garden and find the trap door Hilkiah disappeared through, as well as the one in the hallway. He wondered if the entire complex was honeycombed with secret passageways.

A lad, several years older than the street urchin, entered the garden. He wore a brown robe and had a shaved head. He bowed very low and politely asked Timon to follow, which Timon did as well as KiKu and the "whelp."

The street boy, dazzled that another boy near his age could be in the temple of Bhuttu, asked him endless questions while fingering the material of the robe.

The temple servant ignored him, except to pull his clean robe from the boy's dirty fingers.

KiKu tapped the street urchin on top of his filthy

head and ordered him to behave.

The boy folded his arms and sullenly marched behind KiKu, making faces behind the Bilboa's back.

The temple lad showed Timon to a spacious compartment that provided a balcony overlooking the western portion of the city and the plains beyond the city's walls. As the lad showed Timon his room, several other youths entered with hot water, towels, and bathing oils. A tray of fruit and beverages was provided, as well as a small tunic made of fine cloth and small leather slippers. Timon gave the older of the youths a gold coin, requesting that he wished to make a small donation to Bhuttu for the kindness the priests had shown.

The servant boy tucked the coin in his robe, assuring Timon it would be given to the priest in charge of donations. Timon was sure the coin would find its way to the temple's coffers. The priests of Bhuttu had a reputation for scrupulously honoring their word.

Timon washed his face, hands, and feet. Taking off his clothes, he shook them over the balcony rail to remove the city's dust. Lounging in his loincloth, he ate while watching KiKu struggle to give their young ruffian a bath.

Exasperated, KiKu scraped off much of the city grime with the oils and a bathing pumice. He then examined the boy while drying him. "He seems healthy enough," huffed KiKu, pulling a clean tunic over the boy's head. "No deformities I can see. His teeth are quite good. Still, Madric and Pearl should take a look and examine him for parasites."

"There is nothing wrong with me, Master," pouted the boy. "I'm strong. I will not be a burden. You will see."

"What I see is a very weedy boy whose knees are knobby from the want of good food and whose hair is full of bugs," replied Timon casually.

"Not anymore," boasted KiKu, showing Timon a basin filled with dirty water, which was lined with dead lice and grime.

"Loathsome," replied Timon, motioning for KiKu to remove the basin. He had picked up the Hasan Daegian dislike of anything crawling on the skin. KiKu threw the water over the balcony.

The boy looked disapprovingly at Timon, but remained quiet. He realized he had to stay in Timon's good graces. He tried pulling on his slippers, but couldn't quite get the hang of it since he had never worn a pair of shoes.

KiKu picked up a sharp knife used to cut the fruit and grabbed one of the boy's feet. With the expertise of a skilled surgeon, KiKu began carving away the boy's long and unsightly toe nails while dodging kicks from the other foot. "Be still!" commanded KiKu. "You want to put your new shoes on, don't you!"

Wiping a few tears from his eyes, the boy nodded and remained still for the remainder of the nail carving.

"What's your name, boy?" Timon asked.

"I dunno," replied the boy, not taking his eyes off KiKu wielding the knife.

KiKu shot a small glance at Timon.

"What would you like to be called?" asked Timon, feeling sorry for the boy.

The boy's face lit up. "Something that sounds important."

Timon smiled. "How about Akela?"

KiKu stopped his grooming in surprise.

Akela was Timon's older brother. He had been killed during the siege of Anqara.

KiKu threw the boy's slippers at him. "Our Master has done you a great honor by giving you the name of Akela. Make sure you do not disgrace it."

Akela looked at the grave face of KiKu. "I promise," he replied with much sincerity. "This has been the most wonderful day of my life. On this day, I have a new tunic. I have shoes for the first time in my life. Now I have a name. I belong somewhere." He hugged KiKu's hand.

KiKu jerked his hand away. "You will probably be an ingrate who will show the hangman how to slip the noose over our heads."

Akela shook his head. "I know what this name means. It means honor of the house. It is given to the eldest son in a family," he boasted with pride.

Timon did not see the light in the boy's eyes, as he had turned toward the wall, silently grieving for the loss of his beloved brother.

20

Dorak watched the new arrivals.

Iegani, the Great Divigi of the Dinii, accompanied him.

In the corner of the room sat Timon, KiKu, and a small boy. Recognizing KiKu through his disguise, Dorak seemed puzzled about the other two Bhuttanians.

"Who is the young man?" asked Iegani.

"I haven't seen him since he was a mere lad, but I am positive he is Prince Bes Amon Ptah. I don't know who the little boy is."

"Why would this prince be with KiKu?"

"I don't know. His family is from a powerful tribe living on the Plain of Moab. They have been strongly influenced by the Anqarian culture for centuries until they are not considered true Bhuttanians any longer. His people are monotheistic. They do not worship Bhuttu or any of the lesser gods, so I would say that his presence here is a ruse."

"Undoubtedly," said Iegani, studying KiKu. "That is one of the best disguises I have ever seen him assume."

Dorak grunted. He respected KiKu for his adaptability and skill, but hated him for his betrayal of Zoar and himself by becoming a double spy for Queen Abisola, Maura's mother.

Sensing Dorak's hostility, Iegani said, "Put away your anger, son. We do not have the luxury of it in this place. If KiKu can help us get out of here, then let us not impede his efforts."

Ignoring Iegani, Dorak spread his arms out and closed his eyes. "I feel power."

Iegani shook his wings. "That's because KiKu has Zedek's amulet hidden between his butt cheeks. I can see it in his mind. I wonder why the priests don't realize the amulet is here?"

Dorak's eyes popped open. "We must not let Zedek get close to him!"

"Zedek cannot influence him any more than we can. KiKu is very safe from that old buzzard." Iegani made a few clicks in Dini language and then reverted to Hasan Daegian, which Dorak spoke fluently. "It is the physical world that must be manipulated, and only KiKu and these two boys may do that. Let us hope the gods are with them."

"You don't believe in the gods, Iegani."

"I have been proven wrong about many things in my lifetime. Perhaps I am wrong about the existence of a god."

"May any god take pity on us."

Iegani shrugged. "Or, at least, may She not take pity on Zedek."

21

Timon began his training.

After several days of fasting and passing several oral examinations on religion, Timon was allowed to don the orange robes of a novice. His head was shaved, as was his entire body. He was given a small cell on the bottom floor of a dormitory where older initiates stayed. Timon coped as best he could with the flies and gnats that infested his thin bedding.

Akela and KiKu worked in the kitchen where they proved to be inept and were then made to scrub floors. This is exactly what KiKu wanted as he could closely inspect the hallways for hidden chambers and passages without drawing attention to his crawling around on his knees and tapping the walls. So far he had found three passages, although he had not had the chance to search them.

When opportunity presented itself, he taught Akela some of the techniques of discovering a secret panel or hallway.

Since Akela had the soul of a scoundrel, he picked up information quickly, which pleased KiKu to no end. KiKu thought that if the boy did not betray them or die during the escapade, he might adopt the little urchin since he had no son of his own. His only daughter was grown, and he had not seen her for many years. And so the master spy and the street orphan worked side by side, washing away the dust from polished corridors as they waited for something to happen.

Timon would pass the two, almost envious of their labor, as he was bored to death with the life of a novice. Hour after hour, he studied the religious dogma and traditions of Bhuttu and Bhutta, while forcing his body to obey the rigorous demands of ascetic life. Always, he had been celibate, quiet, and astute. Being a political hostage in the court of Zoar had taught Timon to be unobtrusive and invisible. Timon took pains not to draw attention to himself. He did what he was told and blended in with the other votaries as much as possible.

But life was difficult. Votaries were given only four hours to sleep each night, and their food was mainly fried bread and overcooked legumes. At the end of the day, he was hungry. Timon felt his mind start to go numb from the daily grind, dull food, and deprivation of sleep. Weakened and finding it more difficult to keep his mind on his real objective, Timon wondered if the food was salted with drugs that stupefied his thinking. His already lean body was growing thinner.

Passing KiKu in the hallway one afternoon, Timon sneezed with the dust KiKu and other workers were stirring up. A sneeze was the signal KiKu and Timon had agreed upon if one needed the other.

Reprimanded for making noise, Timon was sent to his cell early that evening without dinner to contemplate on making his body a servant of his mind, not the other way around. Timon weakly crawled onto his pallet and waited for KiKu.

Timon must have fallen asleep for he was awakened by a hand clasped over his mouth. Startled, the votary blinked involuntarily in the darkness as his body tensed, ready to fight. Slowly, the hand loosened until it pulled away.

In the gleam of a single shaft of moonlight illuminating the cell, Timon caught a quick glimpse of KiKu's face. Into Timon's hand was thrust a pouch, and then KiKu was gone.

Timon tucked the pouch between his legs where it was hidden by his manhood, and he bound his loincloth tighter. Its mystery would have to wait until morning when he could see plainly.

Comforted by KiKu's visit, Timon fell to sleep and dreamed he was in Maura's tent sitting on the dais with the empress feeding him from her table of plenty. She even took her napkin and dabbed crumbs from the corners of Timon's mouth. If one chanced upon Timon at that moment, he would have seen a young man curled under a thin coverlet, smiling in his sleep.

22

A sliver of light entered the cell.

It landed on Timon's eyelids. The novice fluttered open his eyes and immediately rooted for his pouch. He had only a few moments. Turning over on his stomach and away from any possible prying eyes, he lifted the pouch to his face and opened the thongs, moving as little as possible. With deft fingers, he pulled out a folded piece of fabric and gingerly undid it.

Written in blood, it read.

DANGER! FOOD POISONED! TAKE
MEDICINE.

Timon turned over the material.

Nothing was written on the back.

Disappointed, Timon cursed, "May his wives have evil odors between their legs." Then Timon thought better of his outburst for he respected KiKu's wives. He wished no harm to them. "May his pecker never straighten to the sun."

Feeling better, he muttered, "No instructions on how to take the antidote or even what it is." Timon gently poured the contents of the pouch into his hand. Out rolled the amulet and several small beeswax pellets wrapped in leaves. He put the powerful amulet aside. He was more interested in something to put in his empty stomach. Timon picked up one of the pellets and smelled it. Unwrapping one, he discovered gray dust. He smelled it again. "Here goes nothing," said Timon as he popped one into his mouth. He collected his saliva and swallowed it. It tasted like mud. Disillusioned, he placed the amulet and the pellets back into the pouch and returned it between his legs.

He hoped his superiors would not search him or the other novices for contraband as they sometimes did. Scrunching up the cloth, he put it in his mouth, and after chewing it, he swallowed it whole as well. The thought that he was putting someone else's blood in his body did not disturb him in the least. Its iron could only help him in his present predicament.

The temple gong sounded, and a whisper of collective moans could be heard from the other cells down the corridor. Each novice staggered out of his small cell and trudged down the hallway with his robe slung over his shoulder. Coming to a larger annex, each man relieved himself in buckets left by the wall and then shuffled over to a long water trough where they shaved their faces and heads.

Drying himself off with his clothes, Timon hurried to the temple where morning devotions were already underway.

Scurrying through the door meant for new votaries, Timon took his place at the back of the temple. Bowing his head and kneeling, he began reciting the liturgy required for morning prayers while sneaking glances here and there. He needed to spend hours in the main temple to study it and perhaps open contact with the lost Dinii. But in his heart, he thought it useless.

For the three weeks he had been training, no one had mentioned any unusual events in the temple complex. No disembodied voices, no ghostly pleas from forgotten overlords of the planet—nothing.

There was neither gossip nor any sightings because this was a wild gootee chase. Resentful that he was being drugged and half-starved, Timon realized he was thinking more clearly. His keen mind was actually working again. Timon attributed it to KiKu's home-made pills.

Timon studied the other devotees milling around

him, unfolding their prayer rugs and laying them neatly out on the marble floor. They were also thin like him, and their eyes had the glazed look of a stunned boaep caught in a lamplight. Timon concluded everyone was being drugged. Timon grunted. This was the time in a novice's life when he ceded his property to the temple. It was obvious the priests deliberately clouded their minds, so the novices would not have second thoughts about signing their wealth over. When the novice awoke from his drugged state, it would be too late. His property would be under the control of the temple, and his relations with the outside world severed. One either complied or committed suicide.

Timon admired their cold and calculating system. Because he had worked as a scribe dealing with property deeds, reports, and accounting records, Timon began to concede that his trip inside the bowels of Bhuttu might not be wasted. If he could locate their records, he could report to the empress the sites of Bhuttu's most important properties where strongholds of rebels could be in hiding. This was something he could use to bargain for his people's lives. Timon's heart leapt. He had hope again.

Hilkiah emerged from the shadows and ascended the altar. He was wearing his priestly robes of black with his elaborate horned headdress with gold feathers.

Another priest wearing a saffron-colored robe walked about the kneeling priests and novices, swinging burning incense, which created a great deal of smoke.

All kneeled on their rugs and smudged themselves with the holy incense as the priest moved past them.

"Peace be with thee, brothers," Hilkiah said.

"Our peace will be found in death," answered the congregation.

"May Bhuttu accept thy final sacrifice."

"May He be kind to thee as well," rejoined the crowd.

Timon felt a tickle on the back of his neck. He ignored it.

After a few minutes of Hilkiah droning on about a priest's responsibilities, Timon felt a tickle again. He twitched his neck a little, hoping to discourage flies. Then Timon felt it again. He was sure he felt the unmistakable breath from another being upon his neck.

Timon searched to the left and right of him. No one was observing at him. Timon reached out slowly behind him, but felt no one crouching behind.

Perhaps KiKu's pellets were inducing hallucinations.

Curse that KiKu! Timon's anger welled up. He decided not to pay any attention to whatever was happening. He did not want to be punished for any indiscretion before he was ready to search for the records hall.

Then something Hilkiah said caught Timon's ear.

"Though only days from our city gates, we, as Bhuttu's servants, must remain calm and meet the nonbelievers with courage and steadfast loyalty to our traditions."

The blood in Timon's veins pulsed faster.

"We will remain in the confines of the temple walls, showing partisanship for neither side. Politics are not our concern except that our faith remain untainted by new ideas and our ways of worship go undisturbed." Hilkiah turned toward the statue of Bhuttu and bowed his head while the acolyte swung his canister of incense around the altar, creating a dreamy effect.

Timon was stunned. He thought he would have more time. Damn that food. It had kept him in a daze, not allowing Timon to work to his full potential. Now Maura was within days of the city, and he was without any proof of the existence of the Dinii or any plan of action! His body felt chilled. He had failed, and his people would be slaughtered!

The former scribe-turned-spy closed his eyes and began formulating plans to outmaneuver the empress. Running away would do no good. She would just take her anger out on his people. His tribe could escape to a new land! No—his people would stand to meet their enemy only to have Maura mow them down like a herd of wild borax browsing on summer grass. Even if he could convince his people to flee, the empress would find them and carry out her threat of annihilation.

Timon had only two options. He must find the Dinii or change Maura's mind if he failed. The problem with the first solution was that he did not believe the Dinii were contained within the walls of the massive temple complex. Maura was simply under a delusion produced by her grief over the loss of her husband.

Without warning, a priest, praying near the base of Bhuttu's statue, let out a blood-curdling scream and threw himself down the altar steps.

Hilkiah sharply turned around. His pink eyes threw off dangerous sparks as he wrapped himself in a protective cloak of angry, red energy.

Timon's lips parted and formed a partial snarl at seeing the protective orb. His people had a deep loathing of magic. Until now, the veneration of Bhuttu had been non-magical and harmless, even with its showmanship and trickery, which could be easily duplicated by any con-man employing his trades in the street. But the swirling cloud about Hilkiah could not be anything but true magic. The sight of it made Timon break into a cold sweat. The use of sorcery was unnatural to him.

The priest, prone on the steps, began babbling.

Its effect on Hilkiah was interesting to Timon. The red cloud surrounding Hilkiah dimmed momentarily before the priest twirled off the altar and into one of the side chambers.

The older priests tried to comfort the frightened priest, who was now gesturing in the air. Many of the novices huddled together in fearful little groups, whispering among themselves.

Timon would not be surprised if some of his brethren would flee into the night if given a chance. The babbling priest was creating a great deal of commotion, and others seemed cowed.

Seeing that no one was paying any particular attention to him, Timon slipped over to the side of the hall and scurried behind tall columns, which supported the stone roof until he was near the massive altar. Peering from behind an ancient tapestry, which divided the altar and the nave, Timon got a good view of the jabbering priest who was still pointing to the ceiling. He looked up to where the priest was pointing and gasped, seeing a disembodied face of a man hovering above him.

Distorted and foggy, it peered downward from the ceiling, and although it seemed to be mouthing words very slowly, nothing could be heard. Pale as Hilkiah, the face's whiteness had an unhealthy likeness to faded parchment, not like skin at all.

The vision grew fainter and fainter.

Everyone gathered in a confused throng at the altar, staring up at the ceiling.

Timon took this opportunity to step out from behind his hiding place and mingle with the rest of the crowd. He pushed through until he reached the rug of the priest, who had first sighted the vision. Hunching down, he pushed feet out of the way and pounded his fist on bare toes to get people to step off the rug. Using his fingertips, he felt the fabric. Nothing unusual there. Next, he lifted up the corner of the rug trying to balance himself against the jostling of the crowd. Knowing he had only a short time before the priests collected themselves and took control again, Timon frantically searched for anything that could explain the vision. Then his hand felt something soft. Pulling it out, Timon tucked it into his robe.

The older priests gathered into a tight little knot and hurled balls of blue energy at the distorted face, which was now barely visible. The blue orbs exploded with a loud blast into the face of the vision. The vision's eyes blinked several times as though surprised, and—then poof—like a puff of smoke from a fire-eater's mouth in the village square, the vision was gone.

Timon rubbed his face and stared at the ceiling, straining his eyes. The vision had indeed disappeared, and nothing remained of it.

The older priests returned their attention to the congregation. They gave the signal to disburse.

Timon had no choice but to leave the sanctuary, but he did not return to his dull little cell. He went to find KiKu. He did not have long before a strong hand reached out from behind a tapestry and pulled him down a secret passage. Timon did not cry out, as he was used to KiKu pulling him into mildewed dark rooms, cold pantries, and stale passageways to talk with him. He thought KiKu gained a perverse pleasure from stealing him out from under the very noses of the watchful priesthood. He merely acquiesced and waited for KiKu's chuckles to die.

Timon usually would not give KiKu the satisfaction of knowing that every time he pulled this stunt, Timon's heart fell to his knees, but Timon was really irritated this time.

"I suppose you know about the vision in the sanctuary." He was tired and wondered if KiKu's medicine was going to sicken him with a side effect.

KiKu's breath was short for he had run very fast. "As soon as I heard the commotion, I came and hid in the sanctuary. There is a spy hole in one of the walls. I saw the last part of the vision."

Timon wiped a spider's web from his ear. "Well?"

"We might not have confirmed the presence of the Dinii, but we have evidence of Zedek."

"Who?"

"The Black Cacodemon, my boy! That was his face you saw. He lives! The empress will not be pleased about this."

Both KiKu and Timon were quiet. KiKu was the first to break the stupor of their private thoughts. "I saw you investigating a rug."

"Oh yes," replied Timon, excitedly. He reached into his robe and searched among the folds. "I found something underneath it."

"What is it?"

"I can't seem to find it," said Timon as he patted himself down. "I must have dropped it in the hallway."

KiKu fell to his knees, searching the floor.

"Wait a minute. Here it is." Timon pulled out a long white feather that had been dyed purple at the very end and sparkled from diamond dust.

KiKu gasped. "By the gods! It is Empress Gitar's." He grabbed the distinctive feather from Timon's hand and smelled it. "It is the genuine article. Smell it," said KiKu, excitedly holding the feather to Timon's face.

Timon wrinkled his nose. "It smells like a marsh."

"Exactly," said KiKu, dancing a little jig. "We have found the Dinii. We have found the Dinii!!!"

"Then we can get out of this hellhole?"

KiKu retorted, "Not exactly. This is but half of our quest. We must now free them, and let us not forget that the Black Cacodemon is with them, wherever they are. If we free them, we might also have to let loose that demon."

"I don't like the sound of that," replied Timon worried. "That's not a good idea. If we let him loose, might Jezra get her hands on him and use him against the Great Mother?"

"We have to take that chance." KiKu was quiet for a moment. "I will send the boy with this feather to my wives. He can slip out of here easily. We have already discovered several tunnels, which lead out of the temple complex. Meanwhile, you and I can work on the means of setting the Dinii free."

Timon shivered. "I do not see how you stand this worrisome intrigue every day. It leaves me cold."

KiKu grinned, but his smile displayed sad overtones. "It's a living."

23

Akela took the torch.

He pressed his thin body through the mouth of the tunnel. Akela had been entrusted with a pouch, and he kept touching it to make sure it still hung by his side, even though KiKu had tied very secure knots to his clothing. One would have to strip the boy naked to snatch the cheap cloth pouch that was an everyday lunch sack. Of course, it was only a decoy. The real feather was tucked in his undergarment, but if anyone bothered to check there, Akela would have more to worry about than just a theft.

Akela made his way along the dirty corridor, occasionally stopping to listen for noise. He passed several doorways while hunting for any telltale signs of recent use. He did not know how he would be able to explain his using the corridor if chanced upon by a priest.

Although his child's mind was surprisingly sophisticated, it was still that of a child's. Akela had to blink away the tears falling from his long eyelashes. He could not remember his mother, but he understood the concept of succor, and to him, that now meant KiKu's wives. He was going to get to them as fast as his little legs would take him. And that was fast by anyone's standards.

He came to a stairwell and paused, listening for anyone coming. Hearing nothing but the sound of his heart beating, he descended, taking care to avoid the crumbling parts of the steps. Reaching the underground floor, he followed the corridor under the bowels of the temple, his feet slapping noisily in the water that bathed the floor. Here the walls were slimy and the air foul smelling. He slipped twice on the grimy mud that had built up century after century upon the stone floor. Akela's feet sank at least an inch into the smelly muck and made a sucking noise as he yanked his foot out of its terrible pull.

Thankfully, the frail boy finally came to some stairs, which took him up another level, but not entirely out of the belly of the temple complex. He had studied with KiKu time and time again the layout of the underground tunnels KiKu had mapped out so far. Akela kept repeating his instructions under his breath until finally he came to a wooden door. Fishing in his pocket, he pulled out a pick KiKu had fashioned for him. With the skill of a professional locksmith, Akela manipulated the lock until he heard a click. He pushed his weight against the door, and to his relief, it creaked open.

Akela quickly found his way through the maze of corridors and out onto the streets of Bhuttani. With the speed of a small bird, he ran through the crooked streets until he came to the inn housing KiKu's wives. He tossed small pebbles at shutters, hoping the women had not moved since he was last with them when he had delivered food with Lord Timon.

Pearl opened the shutters and peered out.

Recognizing her, Akela waved.

Appearing not to notice the small boy, Pearl closed the shutters.

Akela climbed the limbs of an old battered mingo tree and rested in a crook of a limb until the doorkeeper of the inn opened the courtyard door. He shuffled out into the street, dodging carts delivering wine and bread for the morning meals. He grabbed Akela's dangling foot and shook it. Startled, Akela almost fell, but steadied himself. "The lady told me to gather you and feed you breakfast," mumbled the doorkeeper.

The boy eagerly jumped down and ran through the doorway.

Tippu was waiting for him in the main hall with food.

Akela raced to her table and began grabbing gruel with his grimy hands, stuffing it into his mouth.

Tippu watched Akela gobble his gruel while getting a good deal on his face. She noticed that his body looked as frail as ever. "Don't they feed you in the temple?"

"Very little," mumbled Akela, before he shoved more food into his mouth.

Tippu left the table and returned with a bowl full of shaybar, the traditional Bhuttanian drink of boiled milk with borax blood. "Here," she prodded, "this will make little skinny boys fat."

Akela did not need to be coaxed twice. Shaybar was a delicacy that he rarely had in his short life. He gulped down the red shaybar, wiping his mouth with the end of his tunic, and then went promptly back to his gruel, smacking his lips with obvious contentment.

Tippu waited patiently until Akela finished and let out a loud belch. He belched a second time because he liked the sound.

By this time, Tippu's patience had worn thin. "What news from our master?"

Akela blushed and blurted out, "I need to make water."

Tippu sighed and waved her hand toward the out-house. "Go and be quick about it."

The little boy dashed off and extracted his package. He stayed long enough to urinate and then rushed back to Tippu. The young woman, squeamish at the thought of touching the damp cloth, had Akela drop it into her shawl and hurried upstairs to the other wives.

Akela followed closely behind.

Pearl, Madric, and Tippa exclaimed when they saw both the package and Akela.

Pearl took the package and placed it on a table while Madric handed her a sharp knife. She carefully cut the string and unfolded the cloth with the tip of the knife blade.

"Do you know what it is, Akela?" asked Madric, holding her breath.

Akela shrugged his shoulders. "Just some stupid feather."

"A FEATHER!!!" exclaimed the women in union.

Akela's dark eyes widened at their excitement. He nodded.

Pearl hurried until the package was open and ginger-ly pulled out a large white feather with a tip that was partially died purple. "The Dinii," she whispered.

Madric touched the feather. "It is Empress Gitar!"

Tippa and Tippu gathered Pearl's cloak and boots,

while Pearl retied the feather.

Madric produced a small pair of boots for Akela.

He looked at them questioningly.

"Put them on," Tippa requested. "You are going to join Pearl and me."

"Where are we going?" questioned Akela, as he sat on the bed, taking off his worn slippers.

"To see a woman about a large bird," Tippa replied. "Now, hush. We must hurry."

Fear crept into Akela's eyes. "We must be traveling outside the city if you are putting on boots," he said to Tippa. He stared at his feet and suddenly stood up realizing the women's true intention. "I won't go with you!" he exclaimed. "She eats children. I've heard about her. She is a demon. I hear women at the well talking."

"Hush. People will hear you." Tippa boxed Akela's ears and instantly regretted it. She knelt down and clasped a stunned Akela to her small breasts. "I'm sorry, but many people's lives depend on us getting this information to the empress. It is not true what the well women say about her. They are Bhuttanian and fear her because she is Hasan Daegian. I swear to you on my life she will not harm you, but I need—we need you to come with Pearl and me to give witness to what you have learned. Please trust me. You will be safe. Please." She kissed his forehead. "Please."

Shamed, Akela bowed. "My mother is only a little memory. I do not know where she is. I will travel with you, because I do not want to go back to the streets, and I have nowhere else to go."

Pearl, touched by the little boy's speech, placed her rough hand on Akela's shoulder. "You will always have a home with us, Akela."

Akela shook his head. "Master KiKu may not want me."

Madric let out a brittle laugh. "Hittal women decide the children in the family. If we want you, there is nothing he can say. Come now. Dry your tears. Pearl and Tippa must go."

Akela started to blow his nose on his tunic hem until Tippu handed him a clean rag.

All four women kissed him and helped Akela put on his little boots with their breasts grazing his legs and arms. He enjoyed being enveloped in their clean, sweet smell. They gave him new clothes and placed a red wig on his head.

Minutes later, Pearl and Tippa carried their food baskets as though they were trekking to the market for the day's food with their travel bundles secured under their skirts. Pearl had the precious feather under her shirt tucked in her waistband.

Akela acted as their servant.

They gamely marched down the streets to the market while holding their headscarves over their noses to keep out the dust.

Stepping through the doorway of an abandoned house, they quickly shut the door. From large baskets they had placed there previously, they threw off their cloaks and put on the white gowns with the colorful belts belonging to the Siva men. Tippa helped Pearl tie down her breasts and then drape the elaborate headdress around her head. When finished, Pearl looked like any Siva man, which was to say a white enigma. Pearl then helped Tippa.

"What about me?" asked Akela, admiring the beautiful girdles. His face fell when he saw Pearl pull out an ugly black tunic with a rip up the side.

"Sivans don't let their male children out of Siva until they are at least sixteen," Pearl replied. "You will have to travel as a servant's child we are escorting to Hittal."

Disappointed, Akela threw the black tunic over his new clothes but kept his boots on. Before he knew it, he was trotting after two "Sivan men" who walked with quiet purpose.

24

The three joined a Sivan caravan.

It passed through the gates after being inspected by the guards.

Akela was surprised the Sivan men said nothing to the Bhuttanian guards after they discovered three stowaways in their midst. It was only after they were out of sight of Bhuttani that the caravan stopped, and the Sivan leader approached Pearl, Tippa, and Akela.

Both women knelt in supplication. Pearl extended her arm, pulling back the white robe.

All Akela could make out was a henna tattoo, which most Siva men drew on their arms for adornment.

The leader inspected Pearl's henna design without comment. He looked at her and then at Tippa. Finally at Akela. Without warning he grabbed Akela and placed him on the back of a borax cow. Saying nothing to anyone, he strode to the front of the caravan and gave the signal to continue.

For two days, they traveled until they came to a small stream. The leader of the caravan approached Pearl and whispered in her ear.

She nodded and gathered food from the cook's wagon before striking out in an easterly direction.

Tippa and Akela reluctantly followed her into the wilderness, sad to give up the protection of the Sivan caravan.

They walked for several hours under the hot sun until Tippa had to give Akela a ride on her shoulders. They continued, even though they tripped over rocks, bruising their feet. The trio trekked across the edge of the Plain of Moab and could see to the west of them for several miles.

There was nothing, not even a tree, except for scattered clumps of wild yellow grass.

Examining her surroundings, Tippa despaired. She wondered if Pearl was lost. After hours of carrying Akela, Tippa's shoulders ached. She called to Pearl. "I must set the boy down and rest."

Pearl helped the younger woman lower the boy onto the hard-packed terrain. She looked for grass to place on Akela's face to shield him from the blazing sun. Seeing a tall clump of bazera grass, she went over to it and began pulling its long stocks until a hand reached out from beneath the grass and clasped her wrist. Startled, Pearl screamed and tried to pull away.

Akela awoke with a jerk and followed Tippa, who was running toward Pearl. They both stopped short upon seeing a Hasan Daegian woman, camouflaged in bazera grass, step out in front of them.

Still holding Pearl in a tight grip, the scout put two fingers in her mouth and made a bird call. Turning her attention to Pearl, she whispered in Anqarian, "Be quiet," and let go of her wrist.

Minutes later, several Hasan Daegian ponies carrying warriors emerged from the plains. They had been hiding behind a small rolling hill blending into the landscape.

The scout jumped on her horse. She gathered Pearl about the waist and hoisted the woman behind her.

The others followed suit with Akela and Tippa.

Never having seen a Hasan Daegian woman before, Akela was dumbstruck. He had never seen women so big and strong, being used to the smaller Bhuttanian and Hittal women. He pinched the woman in front of him to make sure all that flesh was hers. The warrior turned around in her saddle, giving Akela a fierce look.

The boy lowered his eyes and held tightly onto the scout's belt, as he had never been on a horse before. He watched the tiny hooves of the pony race over the dry, windy plain and felt as though he must be flying. He felt strangely happy and simultaneously terrified at the same time.

They rode for almost an hour until they were beyond the foothills abutting the end of the Plain of Moab.

Akela gauged they were riding northeast.

Without warning, the ponies stopped near a crop of trees. The scouts brusquely told Pearl to dismount, which she obeyed without question. From the midst of the trees, other Hasan Daegian women stole forth, leading out Bhuttanian warhorses.

Akela shrank back against Tippa. He was familiar with the sight of the monstrous horses, but the thought of mounting one chilled him to his dusty boots.

The warriors gestured for Pearl and her companions to mount behind them.

Servants carried wooden steps to one of the prancing horses.

Pearl, without comment, strode up the steps and attempted to raise her leg over the saddle.

The horse was still too high for the middle-aged woman to pull her weight up so several of the soldiers pushed on her backside and lifted her upon the animal. Following Pearl's example, Tippa and Akela gamely walked up the steps and were more successful in mounting the giant horses.

Before they could catch their breath, the steps were taken away, and the soldiers kicked the horses with their heels. The horses reared their front hooves in one mighty salute before trampling the ground before them.

Pearl, Tippa, and Akela fearfully held on, sensing the soldiers did not have total control over the galloping animals.

Tippa pulled her headdress over her nose, protecting her face from clods of dirt thrown up by the pounding hooves. Doing so made her momentarily lose her balance, only to have the Hasan Daegian warrior reach back and pull a dangling Tippa up by the collar of her white kiva.

The Hasan Daegians drove the warhorses hard until Pearl's legs went numb from gripping her horse and Akela's mouth ached from the constant jarring of his teeth.

Without warning, the warhorses slowed to a bouncing trot. This caused the Hittal women and the Bhuttanian boy more discomfort, but it awakened their stuporous minds. They looked about them and saw they were heading toward a small rise.

Pearl strained her eyes. Upon the hill, she saw someone waiting for them and sighed with relief. The horses lurched up the hill and stopped.

A small contingent of Hasan Daegian women dressed in hunting apparel, with pheasants hanging from their belts, grabbed hold of the bridles of the head-tossing, snorting horses.

The mounted Hasan Daegians jumped off and helped their passengers down.

Pearl and Tippa felt their legs quiver while Akela just plopped on the ground. Each was given a waterbag filled with cool, clean water. All three of the adventurers drank with relish and poured water over their dusty faces.

A redheaded Hasan Daegian with thick braids waited patiently until the party quenched their thirst before approaching the group. She spoke in Anqarian. "Have you business with the Hasan Daegians?"

Pearl pulled back the sleeve of her kiva and held out her arm.

The Hasan Daegian saw the secret mark of a spy. She nodded. "Wait here," she ordered before rushing off to a small grove on the other side of the hill.

Hasan Daegian warriors in full military dress stepped out of the copse and searched the trio. Pearl and Tippa did not resist, but held their arms up obligingly.

Akela squirmed and called the women several filthy names he had learned in the bazaar, causing the combat-hardened women to blush. They looked at the boy curiously and muttered about his bad upbringing.

A Hasan Daegian lad appeared. He put his fingers to his lips and motioned to them.

They followed him into the thick of the grove.

Pearl did not see anyone, but felt many eyes upon her and her party. She dare not make a false move, fearing twenty arrows might fly toward her chest. Pearl hoped Akela did not try the Hasan Daegians' patience. She knew the Hasan Daegians loved children but would not hesitate to run a sword through the boy's side if he was perceived a threat.

The Hasan Daegians were no longer idealists. They had been hardened by years of war.

The lad stopped and turned to Pearl. "Enter the veil. It will not hurt you."

Pearl was confused. She saw nothing but endless trees. "Forward?" she asked.

The lad nodded.

Summoning up her courage, Pearl strode forward, only to pass through something that felt vaguely wet and silky. The sensation startled her, and she stopped only to have Tippa bump into her. "Goodness!" blurted Pearl, stumbling.

Strong hands reached up and helped stabilize Pearl.

"Thank you," said Pearl, catching a glimpse at the helper's hands. She gasped. The hands were blue.

"Goodness, goodness," she gushed. She immediately knelt as did Tippa.

"Forgive me, Great Mother," Pearl said kowtowing.

"Pearl, isn't it?"

"Yes, Great Mother," Pearl replied.

"And you are Lady Tippu."

"Tippa, Great Mother."

They could hear Akela yell, "I'm not going in there. My mothers disappeared. YOU CAN'T MAKE ME!!!" An exasperated Hasan Daegian soldier tried to calm Akela.

"It seems your companion is reluctant," commented Maura.

"Yes, Great Mother," replied both women with their foreheads still touching the ground. They heard Maura move closer to the veil and reach beyond it. There was a rush of air followed by a loud thump. Out of the corner of her eye, Pearl saw an astonished Akela pick himself off the ground and charge the woman in front of him dressed as a hunter. He did not seem to notice or was too frightened to care that the woman's skin was blue.

Pearl closed her eyes, expecting the worst. She saw the woman reach out and pull Akela up into the air by his loose clothing. He tried to kick her, but couldn't reach with his feet.

A soldier rushed in and grabbed the little boy into a headlock.

Akela could not move. His feet dangled uselessly.

Maura cautioned, "Little boy, I do not know who you are, but if you don't show some manners, the good woman who is holding you will take you away and give you a thrashing you will never forget. She has three children of her own and knows what to do with little boys who irritate their queen and empress." Seeing she had Akela's attention, Maura pressed forward. "If you give me your word as a gentleman and promise to do everything Lady Pearl tells you, my guard will put you down. Blink if you agree."

As his throat was held in the iron grip of his captor, Akela had no choice but to blink.

Maura commanded, "Let him go."

The guard gently put Akela down and stifled a laugh as she saw the boy insinuate himself between the kowtowing Pearl and Tippa.

"You stupid boy," Pearl hissed. "Don't you see who this is? Keep still if you value our lives."

Akela shrugged his bony shoulders while lowering his head like his two companions.

"Tell me your news," ordered Maura harshly. Inside her chest, Maura's heart was pounding. She prayed she would not be disappointed with this Hittal woman.

"Great Mother," said Pearl. "I have something I think will interest you."

Maura barked impatiently, "Show me quick then."

Pearl quickly pulled on a string from around her waist, exposing a pouch. She handed it over.

Maura carefully took the pouch and turned away from the spies and her guards. She opened it up and peered inside. Gingerly, her calloused fingers reached into the darkness of the pouch and took hold of a stem. She slowly pulled out the object and stared at it for a moment. She held the feather aloft and observed its sparkling reflection in the sun's rays. "Great Goddess, it is the feather of a Dini! A royal Dini!"

Maura turned toward Pearl, extending the feather before her. "It is from Gitar!"

Pearl breathed with relief, peeking at Tippa.

A broad smile covered Tippa's face.

The empress had identified that the feather was from Gitar, Empress of the Dinii and Overlord of Kaseri.

They were on the road to being saved from Maura's edict and might yet cheat death.

Maura was drunk with joy. "Tell me! Tell me quick! How did you come to find this?"

"Our young friend can tell you better than I," replied Pearl, nudging Akela.

Akela looked up at the beaming empress and ventured a smile.

"Who are you, young squire?"

"My name is Akela, and I am from the household of Timon de Berechial from Qued Zum. I am his manservant," he boasted proudly.

"Really," replied Maura, observing the little boy kneeling before her. "Well, Timon is my servant, so that makes you my servant as well."

Akela's smile disappeared. He did not like that idea at all.

"I can see it gives you pause." She bent over into the little boy's face. "I give Timon and KiKu pause, so your response better be good. Now tell me the truth, boy. How did you get ahold of this feather?"

Akela pulled away from Maura's feral eyes. He did not like this woman towering over him. "Master Timon found it under a priest's prayer mat in the temple of Bhuttu."

"When?"

"Four days ago. KiKu gave it to me and told me to escape through the tunnels underneath the temple grounds. From there I was to find his wives. They have brought me here. That is all I know. Honest."

"Did KiKu have a message for me?"

"He said something strange about a bluebird needing to protect its own." He shook his head. "I don't remember all of it."

"A bluebird that sings all day and does not stay in the nest will die with the rest."

"Yes, that is it." Akela looked happily up at the woman, but she was not smiling.

"Tippa, take your young friend and pass back through the veil. Have the guards give you something to eat."

"Yes, Great Mother." Tippa paused for a moment.

As if reading her thoughts, Maura said, "Pearl will follow later."

Tippa's face relaxed, and she rose, gathering Akela by the hand. They passed through the veil, hesitating only for a moment.

Pearl could see them, but they were muted and indistinct.

"Please speak, wife of KiKu. I haven't much time."

Pearl glanced uneasily at the veil.

"They cannot hear nor see us," offered Maura. "No one can."

Pearl opened her mouth only to shut it quickly again.

Maura took note of her confusion and let out a low chuckle. "I know what you must be thinking. We Hasan Daegians do not practice magic, so how did we get a security veil? You must be tired. Rise and sit."

Pearl hesitated.

"Please, Lady Pearl. We are old friends, are we not? Let's dispense with the formalities."

Maura handed Pearl a wine goblet after helping her onto a stool. Pearl was glad to get off her knees and drank heartily. The wine contained a stimulant, which started to work immediately. She looked questioningly at Maura. It was very similar to one she had given Timon.

"Mingo bark mixed with pemh grass. No side effects," comforted Maura, trying to reign in her impatience. After all, Pearl had traveled a great distance and had put her life at risk to carry a message to her.

Pearl closed her eyelids and enjoyed the delicious effect of renewed energy and well-being. Suddenly, she jerked forward. "OH, THE MESSAGE!" she blurted. "Please forgive me, Great Mother." She leaned toward Maura's ear. "The Dini feather was found in Bhuttu's temple as Akela told you. It was discovered under the mat of a priest by Timon, during worship where the wizard Zedek appeared before the congregation. He was trying to speak, but no one could hear his message. At least, that is what everyone claimed. KiKu believes the Dinii are held captive with Zedek and possibly Dorak as well."

Maura held up her hand in disbelief. "This is impossible. Zedek is dead. I know for I killed him."

Pearl licked her lips and proceeded with caution. "The sighting was confirmed by many. Zedek appeared to the congregation of Bhuttu and tried to speak with them. It was no trick. Even the High Priest became unsettled and fled."

Maura ran her hand through her dark blue-black hair, thinking of all the possibilities. "What do Timon and KiKu propose to do?"

"They are waiting for your instructions, Great Mother."

"What of Jezra?"

"She is biding her time until you strike. All of the storage houses have been filled with grain, and her soldiers exercise battle drills daily."

"And Cappet and Prosperot?"

"Prosperot is neutral. Cappet will side with the victor. My advice, Great Mother, is to get in contact with Cappet. Bribe him whatever the cost. Give him and his band of criminals immunity for all I care, but get him on our side."

"I want all the gates opened upon my signal. Do you think this Cappet could manage it?"

"It will take much gold, but I think he could arrange it. He has many men under his control. Even Jezra dare not confront him."

"Good. I will have our people inside the city contact him."

Pearl asked, "We have more spies inside the city?"

"You didn't think I would let Timon and KiKu go in Bhuttani alone, did you? KiKu never dismantled his spy network. They are still working, but reporting to a different master."

"I didn't realize."

"Take this emerald and gold bracelet," said Maura, pulling off her gold cuff. "It has my royal seal on it. KiKu's people will recognize it."

"Yes, Great Mother. Thank you," said Pearl, hiding the bracelet in her undergarments.

"Tonight, you will rest. Tomorrow, you will return to the city with another Sivan caravan. I will give you a message before you leave on how to use the amulet to free the Dinii. I dared not give it to them before in case they were captured. Do you understand?"

Pearl looked anxiously past the veil.

Maura understood the Hittal's fear. "The boy and Tippa will remain with me. They need not be in Bhuttani during the coming weeks, and you will travel faster without them. Once you have delivered your message, you shall return to me with Madric and Tippu. Timon and KiKu will have to manage on their own the best they can."

"I will need the boy, Great Mother."

Maura thought for a moment. "Alright, but Tippa

will remain as my 'guest.'"

"I understand, Great Mother."

Maura stood.

Pearl immediately jumped to her feet and bowed. When Maura did not speak again, Pearl raised her head and found the empress was gone. Pearl shook her head and passed through the humming veil. There she saw Tippa and Akela eating with gusto while the guards raised a water vessel in a tree so they might bathe.

Akela smiled at Pearl and waved her over. "Look at all of the food!" Akela exclaimed with his mouth crammed full of cakes.

A senior officer approached Pearl with a tray heaped with food.

Pearl thanked her while noticing the woman's high rank.

"A Sivan caravan will pass several miles from here tomorrow. You are to join them and pass through to the city again. As soon as you deliver your message, you are to rejoin our empress."

"How will I find her?"

The officer smiled. "An army of fifty thousand people is hard to miss. You will find us. After you have eaten, we have prepared water for bathing."

"Are we not to return with you?" asked Tippa of Pearl.

"You are to be a guest of the empress until your friend returns to us," said the officer.

"Oh, I understand," Tippa whispered.

"I thought you might," replied the guard softly. She turned her attention to Pearl. "After you have eaten and bathed, a clean Sivan robe will be provided for you. A tent is waiting when you wish to retire," she said, pointing.

Pearl turned and looked at the sumptuous tent awaiting.

"A healer will join you later and rub herbs into your feet. They must be sore."

"Thank Her Majesty for such accommodations. We appreciate her thoughtfulness," Pearl stated, weary from all the intrigue.

The senior officer kindly touched Pearl's arm. "The war cannot last forever, and then we will all go back to our lives."

Pearl nodded in concurrence, hoping with all her heart the Hasan Daegian officer was right.

25

Maura pulled her horse to a stop.

There it stood—Bhuttani in all its foreboding glory. Dusty, gloomy, and formidable.

It was nothing like the graceful and beautiful city of O Konya.

Bhuttani stood like a hard knot upon the land. As the first rays of the sun stole across the plain on which the capital stood, Maura could see its massive walls needed repair. The city was decaying from a lack of leadership.

Maura smirked and quickly replaced her expression with a dour expression. She did not want the Bhuttanians to see her gloating at the sight of their beloved capital in such disrepair.

In her heart of hearts, she wanted to put a torch to it and burn it to the ground, but she now would have to rebuild it if her daughter was to become aganess.

The Bhuttanians were leeches upon the rest of the world, and they would have to be contained with a firm hand in order for the land to recover. Maura was determined they would never gain the upper hand again. She glanced at Alexanee.

His face was ashen as he stared at his beloved capital. Always before, Alexanee had wondered if he was doing the correct thing by throwing his effort behind Maura and not Dorak's first wife, but now he saw he had been right in his judgment.

Jezra had let the city deteriorate into such a state that capturing it would not take long.

Disgusted, Alexanee gave the signal for the soldiers to surround the city.

When his fellow Bhuttanians awoke this morning, they would find a massive army of their fellow Bhuttanians and Hasan Daegians standing with a mishmash of Anqarians and mercenaries from every country the Bhuttanians had conquered, waiting to exact a painful retribution upon the city. He prayed Jezra would have the sense to surrender or else much blood would be spilled.

A courier rushed a message to Maura.

She bent down, grabbing the message and dismissing the young woman.

Alexanee looked on as Maura broke open the sealed scroll. "What does it say?"

Maura quickly read that coded message. *The boy and the woman have made it into the city unharmed. The boy is in the temple.* She replied, "It states that Cappet has agreed to our terms."

The general bowed his head. "Everyone is moving into place."

"His men will open the western gate when we give the signal."

"What did we promise him?"

"A percentage of all tax on river trade in the Bhuttanian Empire."

Alexanee chuckled. "He's not a thug. He's a business man."

Maura nodded. "If he survives the attack, Cappet will become a very wealthy man."

"And he will keep the eastern gate open, too?"

"The gate will stay open as ordered. He is letting out as many civilians as possible. We have people stationed intercepting them."

"Yes, I want to make sure Jezra and Mikkotto don't flee the city hiding with the refugees."

"Make sure you search for that boy of Jezra's. She might send him out alone with a trusted servant."

"Your will be done, Great Mother."

Maura studied her army spreading across the great plain surrounding Bhuttani. Win or lose, today would be the day of reckoning. Both she and Bhuttani would be judged.

As Maura and Alexanee considered the city, a swoosh sounded. The horses bucked while whinnying and snorting loudly.

Something soft brushed Alexanee's face. After getting his horse under control, Alexanee regarded the sky. "Don't shoot! Don't shoot!" he cried to his men, watching a contingent of huge birds fly away.

Maura's war steed had run off, but a soldier captured it and brought it back.

The saddle was empty, and Maura was nowhere to be found.

26

Maura controlled her trembling.

Almost in shock, she checked herself for wounds where claws had pinched her.

A hand gave her a skin of water.

"I can't believe it!" she cried, not yet looking into the face of the Dini standing before her.

"Please calm yourself," spoke a familiar voice.

"Is it you, Benzar?" whispered Maura, grabbing his hand and feeling his feathers. "Is it really you? I thought you were with Empress Gitar." Overcome, Maura began to cry.

"Now. Now," comforted Benzar. "Don't cry, little sparrow. I guarded the hallway and was never in the Mother Bogazkoy's chamber." He patted her back.

"Where have you been?" Maura stared at the rest of the Dinii standing in a little knot surrounding them.

"Why haven't you helped me? Gitar? Is Gitar here? We thought she might be in Bhuttani. I'm so confused."

Maura grabbed Benzar around his waist and hugged him, taking in his familiar Dinii scent. "I searched everywhere."

Benzar patted Maura's head. "All will be explained to you. We haven't much time. Please stop crying. Compose yourself."

The other Dinii nodded their heads in agreement. It grieved them to see Maura so distressed.

Maura pulled away, wiping her eyes. She reached for a handkerchief inside her vest.

Benzar squatted so he could be on eye level with Maura. "Someone is here to see you, little sparrow. Chaun Maaun."

Maura gave a start. "Oh, he can't kill me now. Not on the eve of victory!"

"He is not here to harm you. He wants to find his mother. We think she is held in Bhuttani." Benzar smiled. "But Chaun Maaun will explain all to you. Will you agree to see him?"

"Do I have a choice?"

Benzar grinned, shaking his head. "Not really. It will be fine. You'll see. Ready?"

Maura nodded.

Benzar offered Maura a comforting smile and gave

the signal for his group to fly away.

Maura watched them disappear into the sky.

"Maura?"

The empress swung to see Chaun Maaun standing ten feet from her. She pulled a knife from her leggings. "Stay where you are."

Chaun Maaun stared at Maura with curious detachment. "You look handsome, Maura. Fit and comely. Your skin is noticeably darker. You must have the Bogazkoy with you." He stepped closer.

Brandishing her knife, Maura commanded, "That's far enough. I'm on the verge of capturing Bhuttani. You must not stop me."

Chaun Maaun laughed. "I have no intention of stopping you. In fact, I'm going to help you."

"Help? Why?"

"I think Mother may be in the temple of Bhuttu."

"I think that, also. Why do you?"

"From the reports you have been getting." Chaun Maaun laughed at Maura's confusion. "We have been following you all along. You know how silent we can be. We just fly in and listen to the conversations in your tent."

Maura gave a look of disbelief. "I would have known if a Dini was there. I would have smelled you.

Felt you."

"But you didn't. You have been preoccupied with your new baby and all your lovers. We were with you, Maura, and you didn't even know it. We watched in the woods where you had your uultepes dispatch that poor man. We watched KiKu smuggle Prince Bes Amon Ptah away from the scene. We watched you fake your injuries. Yes, we have been witness to many things."

"What do you propose now?"

"A truce. We help you take over Bhuttani, but our main goal is the temple of Bhuttu. I want to search for my mother and kinsmen."

"What if you find Dorak?"

"Dorak. Always Dorak." Chaun Maaun spat out the words as though spitting out something rotten. "If he has helped my kinsmen, then we will spare him. If my mother tells me he has harmed my people, then I shall kill him. I cannot believe you are still concerned with his welfare. Don't you have a daughter to put on a throne regardless of Dorak? Priorities, Maura. Priorities."

"I have your word you will not fight against me and, once the city is taken, you will fly away without exacting revenge?"

"My people and I will go away if Gitar is found. Alive or dead, we will go away. But remember this,

Maura, you and your people may go back to Hasan Daeg. We will uphold the treaty between our peoples, but if you or any other of your kind enter the Forbidden Zone, then we will have war, and we will destroy your threat for good."

"Only the Forbidden Zone. What about the City of the Peaks?"

"I hope to never set eyes upon it again. You may have it." Chaun Maaun gave a bitter laugh. "That is all I have to say. I leave you now. After this is over, I hope never to see you again."

Maura fell to her knees, reaching out to him. "I loved you. I truly did and still do. You must believe that. I never stopped loving you. I wish things had been different, but my love for Dorak is something that I can't control. The heart desires what it wants."

"Yes, how well I know."

"Even if war had not come, our people would never have allowed us to marry. Surely you must see that now. We never had a future."

"The Dinii will fly into camp before the battle. Send a flaming arrow into the sky when ready for us. We will come. We will come." Chaun Maaun stretched his mighty wings and flew into the oncoming rays of the sun.

"CHAUN MAAUN, WHY WON'T YOU FOR-GIVE ME?" screamed Maura, shielding her eyes against the brightness of the rising sun as she watched Chaun Maaun disappear.

Epilogue

Maura stood on a ridge.

She would lead the charge if the city did not surrender.

Beside her sat Alexanee on a horse overlooking Bhuttan.

Everyone was in place—the cavalry, the archers, the infantry, and the catapults to break down the walls.

Alexanee glanced at Maura.

Maura nodded.

Alexanee gave his prancing white horse a small nudge, and it danced to the front of the line. The cavalry fell in behind him as drummers began to beat loudly on their instruments.

A trumpet blew, giving the signal.

The battle had begun.

Bhuttani would fall before nightfall.

READ ON FOR A SPECIAL PREVIEW!
WALL OF VICTORY
The Princess Maura Tales
Book 5

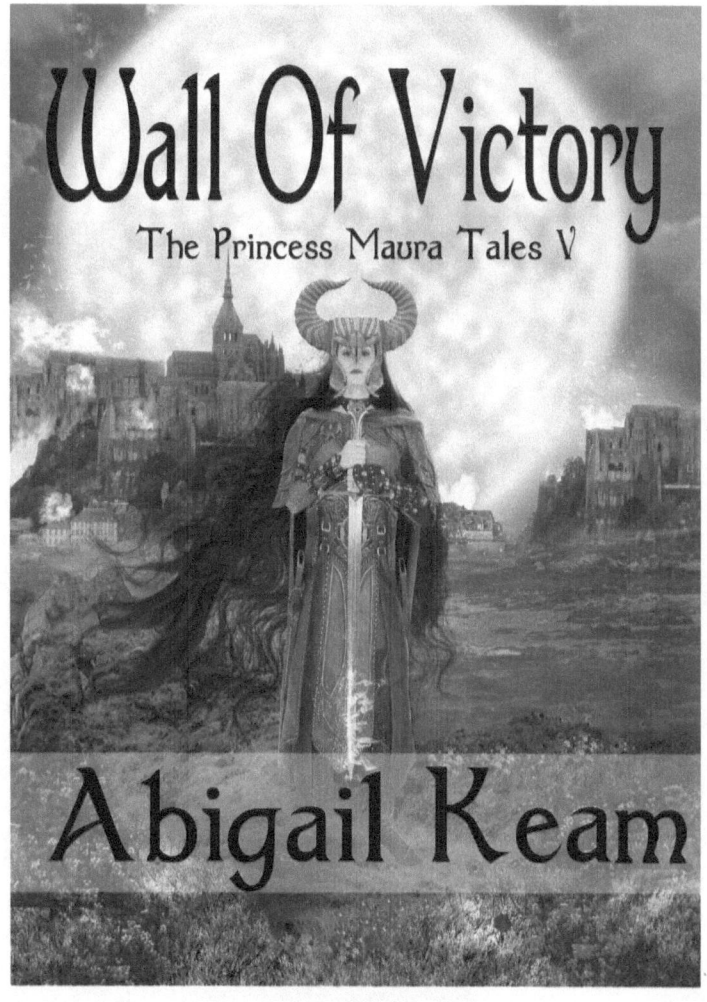

1

War!

War came to Bhuttani.

The city, which had wreaked brutal destruction upon Kaseri, was now facing its own ruin.

The great warrior Maura de Magela was coming to claim the throne of the aga with a coalition of battle-hardened Bhuttanians, Hasan Daegians, Anqarians, Camaroons, and mercenaries from within the Empire.

At first, Bhuttanians refused to believe their kinsmen would take up arms against them, but as terrified refugees fled the countryside and flooded the great city with stories of mighty machines which caused the earth to tremble, soldiers as numerous as the stars in the heavens, and a queen with blue skin and unforgiving eyes who pressed relentlessly toward the capital of Bhutan, citizens began to wonder.

"The Blue Queen wants revenge for the death of her parents," they lamented.

Others speculated that she wanted to place her daughter by Dorak in the Bhuttanian Royal Palace.

Still, many carried on as though nothing would interfere their comfortable lives, believing a Bhuttanian soldier would never fight against his own people. "How can a mere girl harden the hearts of Zoar's men against their kinsmen?"

The refugees babbled, "That she-devil sits upon Zoar's throne of bones atop a great platform dragged across the plains by many beasts. Sitting with her are two great felines which act as bodyguards. She is stronger than any giant and swifter than any bird."

"Nonsense," laughed people in the marketplace as they listened to the wild tales of the frightened newcomers.

"You'll see. You'll see," warned the refugees as they begged for food. "The Hasan Daegian women are tall like our men and as strong too. They have no mercy, obeying their queen without question. Even the noble General Alexanee is at her beck and call. The White Queen is no match for the Blue Queen. We'll all be dead before the seasons change."

Many threw coins at the refugees, shaking their heads in disbelief, but as more exiles flooded the city with similar tales, the people became restless and took to the ramparts to study the horizon.

Could it be true? Could a vast army be coming to exact vengeance? Could the Blue Queen raze Bhuttani as they had leveled Anqara?

They didn't have long to ponder.

One night the lookouts spied pinpoints of distant light. Many said it was the fires of the Blue Queen's camp getting closer and closer. Others remarked it was merely the reflection of a moon upon rocks, but all Bhuttanians went to bed troubled and restless.

The next morning their worries intensified when a cloud of dust and smoke spanning many miles arose along the searing horizon across the plain.

A Sivan caravan entered the city with alarmed traders claiming a vast army was burning every house, every barn, every village across a ten-mile swath, while commandeering everything of value and killing anyone who resisted. "The Great Mother is determined to bring Bhuttan to its knees and the capital Bhuttani along with it. Get out while you can," the Sivans advised the terrified citizens.

While many gathered around for news, no one noticed two "Sivans" leaving the caravan and throwing off their desert robes in an alley.

Now dressed as Bhuttanians in ballooning pants and

dark tunics, Pearl and Akela raced toward the temple.

Bedlam had descended into the heart of the city, with merchants closing shops, soldiers marching toward the western gate, and people hoisting children and possessions on their backs, hurrying to escape.

Pearl wrestled through the crowd, holding Akela's hand. The escaping throng of citizens grew so unruly, she finally had to pick up the small boy and run with him in her arms. Reaching the portico of an abandoned house, Pearl stopped to rest. She heard looters already at work inside. Putting Akela down, she looked carefully behind her. The last thing she needed was a thug hitting her on the back of the head and stealing Akela for the slave trade.

Pearl squatted down to Akela's level. "Akela, we are only two streets from the temple. You must go and give Empress Maura's message to KiKu. Do you think you can sneak back in?"

Akela glanced at the multitude of people scurrying along the street. He nodded at Pearl with resolve. "I can, Mistress. I know I can."

"Good boy. Repeat the message."

Akela parroted the message that had been drummed into him during the journey back to Bhuttani.

Pearl nodded with relief. "Yes. That's it. Now you must give the message to KiKu and then make your way to the east gate, where the Sivan caravan will be waiting. Can you do that for me?"

Akela nodded, his eyes wide.

"I must go to the inn and collect Madric and Tippu. We will meet at the Sivan caravan. You must be there before the sun vanishes tomorrow or the caravan will leave without you. Do you understand, Akela?"

"I will give the message to KiKu and meet you at the east gate before the sun sets."

"Yes, tomorrow. Do you understand what will happen if you fail to meet us?"

Akela remained silent, thinking of the possibilities.

Pearl grabbed his shoulders. "You will be stuck in this city during the attack. Many people will die if they don't get out. You must be by the east gate by dark tomorrow. Promise me you will be there."

Akela looked into Pearl's worried face and saw the mother he never had, but desired. "I will be there, Mistress. I promise."

Pearl gave a wisp of a smile and kissed the top of Akela's head. "Blessings upon you, child. Be off with you now, and be safe."

Akela judged a space in the crowds where he could push his way through. Within seconds, he was swallowed up by the sea of people scrambling for their lives.

Pearl hoped she would live to see Akela again.

Taking a deep breath, she pressed her way into the mob, hoping to find Madric and Tippu safe at the inn. She had to get them out of this city.

Hopefully, KiKu and Timon would be successful in their endeavor. If not, she wondered if the Great Mother would be merciful to KiKu's wives.

One could always wish.

2

Akela pressed through.

He made his way through the city, ducking between legs and squeezing through the crowds until he came to the temple. Hiding behind a refuse bin, he waited until dark. By this time soldiers had established order, and the streets were mostly deserted. Akela stole out from the shadows and scampered into the temple using the route he had taken to escape. Pausing only long enough to allow his eyes adjust to the dim light, he crept along the dark and moldy walls, desperate to make his way to KiKu and deliver the message.

Finding the small oil lamp he had stashed on his way out, Akela fished for the flint he had hidden behind some loose bricks. It took him several minutes to get the damp wick to ignite from striking the flint, but he finally managed. Though the flame from the oil lamp was dim, it illuminated enough to allow Akela to hurry along the damp passageways to KiKu's sleeping room near the wine cellar. KiKu had convinced the priests he could kill more rats if he slept where they kept their nests. They agreed and allowed KiKu to move his pallet into the cellar.

Akela found KiKu resting on his mat near the wine vats. "Master! Wake up!" Akela said while pulling back the ragged blanket, only to find rushes bundled together to resemble a sleeping person.

A hand reached out of the shadows and covered Akela's mouth. "Hush! Do you want to wake the entire complex?"

Akela pulled away from the hand. "Everyone is asleep," he protested, turning to look at KiKu.

"You can never tell who might be listening." KiKu shoved the boy onto his pallet and bit his lip in exasperation. "Akela, tell me the news before I rip out your liver."

Akela gulped. "We met the blue lady with the fancy title. Pearl was afraid of her, I could tell. That made me afraid as well. I didn't like her. Not Pearl, I mean. The blue lady. She didn't have kind eyes."

"Yes, yes, yes," KiKu sighed impatiently. "What did the blue lady say?"

"She kept Tippa, and that made Pearl sad."

"Just tell me what the blue lady *said*, you damned impertinent child!"

Akela sucked in his breath. "Pearl says the empress will strike at the first quarter of the second moon, and you are to get the birds out at all costs. Destroy the temple if you have to, but get them out."

KiKu paced back and forth in his cramped chamber. Stopping suddenly, KiKu grabbed the little boy. "What took you and Pearl so long to get back? Don't you realize our time has all but run out?"

Akela tried to turn his head to escape KiKu's fierce gaze, but KiKu held him so tightly he couldn't. "The caravan had a hard time getting through because of all the people on the roads. There was much thievery and mayhem. With my own eyes, I saw bandits kill an old woman over a bowl of soup. We had to take the long route around."

KiKu exhaled deeply, nodded, and loosened his hold on the boy. "I understand, Akela. I didn't mean to criticize. It's that time is of the essence, but you wouldn't understand, would you? How can a mere boy realize what is at stake?"

"I understand I might get killed."

KiKu chose to ignore Akela's last statement. "Did the blue lady say how we are to use the amulet?"

Akela recited Pearl's message. "As I am blue, press

the stone of the same hue and 'will it.'"

"Will it?"

Akela's eyes grew large at KiKu's menacing expression. "Honest. That's all Mistress Pearl told me to say."

KiKu didn't like the way the boy's eyes darted away from him. "You wouldn't be holding back information for some gold coins?"

"I swear on my mother's grave, that is the message." Akela turned away, but KiKu gripped his arm.

"You little liar. Your mother is probably not dead, and Bhuttanians don't have graves."

"Well, if Bhuttanians don't have graves, what is General Prosperot guarding, then?" asked Akela, drawing himself up.

"Shrines, you fool. Don't you know the difference between a grave and a shrine?"

The boy shook his head. He did not understand why KiKu should be so mean to him when he had risked his life to help. Akela believed he had been very brave, so why was KiKu treating him harshly?

This was the way of the Hittals. They were opportunists with little innate sense of loyalty. Yes, Akela recognized who was standing before him. A man so important that the White Queen would pay handsomely to find him. He could turn KiKu in for a neat profit and buy food for many months.

KiKu's grabbed Akela's throat. "Don't even think it, boy."

"I don't know what you mean," Akela wheezed, grasping at KiKu's iron fingers.

"If I go down, so do the women."

Akela pulled away, rubbing his throat. "I still don't know what you're talking about." Akela was astonished that he could have such a thought. He had come to give the message and then escape with KiKu's wives, who were waiting for him even now. KiKu was right. To betray KiKu was to betray the women, and this Akela would never do. He wanted nothing more than to leave this horrid city before it was overrun with grief and bloodshed. "I would never betray you!"

KiKu grimaced. "One rat recognizes another." He released his grip and tousled the boy's hair. "Stay out of trouble, my young friend. We might make something out of you yet."

Gulping, Akela wondered how long it would be before he could sneak out of the temple and rejoin Pearl.

It couldn't be soon enough for him.

3

T imon was incredulous.

"That's all she had to say? Press the blue stone and 'will it?' Why didn't she tell us this before? We had the amulet and could already have summoned them."

"Perhaps Maura didn't trust us with the information and waited until she had proof the Dinii were in the temple."

Timon curled his hands into fists. "She thought we would betray her to Jezra."

"It was safer if we did not know how to make use of the amulet."

"Who else knows?"

"Until now, only she and the Black Cacodemon knew how to summon the powers of the amulet. The various stones on the amulet command different abilities."

"Such as?"

"I wouldn't know. She didn't entrust that information to me."

"Liar!"

KiKu shrugged. Knowing Timon's nerves were raw, he took no offense at the insult. "The Great Mother and her army will be here within hours, and she wants the Dinii freed. I don't think she's prepared for a long siege. She wants to capture the city quickly."

"Well, why doesn't she ask for one of the moons while she's at it!" Timon uncurled his fists and threw up his hands in disgust.

"She must have identified the feather we sent. We know the Dinii are here. We need to release them. The lives of my wives depend upon it."

"Threats. Threats. Always threats. Why don't we leave? Disappear with the fleeing crowd?"

KiKu drew back. "Too many depend upon us. Besides, Maura would search the world to find us. No, we must do this. We must go to the great hall. That's where the Black Cacodemon was sighted, and where you found the feather."

"What if we release him as well as the Dinii?"

"We must try to kill him. He must not be allowed to come to Jezra's aid."

Resigned to his fate, Timon sighed. "Let's go to

work then. I want to get out of here as soon as possible. This place gives me the chills." He extended his hand. "Give it here."

KiKu blinked at Timon's hand. "Give what here?"

"The amulet, of course."

"I don't have the amulet. I gave it to you."

Timon's eyes widened. "What do you mean? I don't have it. When I awoke, it was gone. I thought you took it for safekeeping."

Timon searched beneath the frayed blanket and tore open the crude straw pallet on KiKu's bed.

KiKu strode around the room at a frantic pace. "Amulets don't get up and walk away!"

"No, they don't, loyal Bilboa, but they can be summoned."

KiKu and Timon looked up to see Hilkiah standing in the doorway. Their eyes caught a multi-colored glimmer below Hilkiah's collarbone.

Timon let out a loud groan.

Hilkiah was wearing the amulet.

A crooked smile spread across the priest's face. "I see thou both dost recognize the sacred amulet. It belongs to Zedek, my mentor and sponsor into the great society of Bhuttu. All magical objects can be summoned. I have felt its presence since ye both joined our community. It has been calling to me in my dreams.

I knew it had to be somewhere in the temple.

"Thou needn't be so aghast, Bilboa. I could have been an apprentice to a cheese guild or a wine merchant or a royal scribe of the Blue Queen, but here I am instead, ready to help my Master."

KiKu murmured to Timon. "That's the extent of Bhuttanian wit for you."

Hilkiah cast a baleful scowl at Timon. "Thou dost not remember me, Prince Bes Amon Ptah, but I remember thee at the court of Zoar. It was just a few occasions when I had to bless something or other at the palace, but thee and thy older brother were present. Just a little thing thou wast, but thee had a peculiar mark on the side of thy neck like this one."

He pointed a finger at a small flower-shaped mole on the back of Timon's neck. "How unfortunate for thee that all novices must shave their hair."

"I don't know what you're talking about, Priest. I am Timon de . . ."

Hilkiah waved his hand. "Save thy breath, young prince. I make no mistake." He slowly inched closer to KiKu. "I am puzzled about thee, though I think thou wast Zoar's man. I never got a good look, as thou wast always lurking in the shadows just out of sight."

KiKu struck his hand out quickly, but Hilkiah jerked his head back. KiKu's hands were met by an angry purple shield, stinging him terribly. He jumped, cradling his singed hand. "Damn you, Priest!"

Hilkiah turned to Timon. "Well, it is clear this man is no Bilboa. It doth not matter. We shall soon have the truth out of thee."

"What do you mean?" Timon asked.

"He means you are going to tell us everything hidden inside your insipid skull," said Mikkotto, stepping into the small sleeping cell.

Timon's eyes narrowed. "Who are you?"

Mikkotto lounged against the doorjamb, slapping her gloves against her thigh. She righted herself and strode over, pressing her lean body against him.

"Stay away. Don't touch me," squeaked Timon.

"Settle down," purred Mikkotto as she stroked the boy's cheek. She leaned into Timon's face until her lips glanced off his. "Very comely in the face. I did not expect you to be so appealing, but you are a tad thin for my taste." Mikkotto's eyes unhurriedly traveled down Timon's body as her hands wandered below his waist.

Timon recoiled from her touch.

Chuckling, Mikkotto reached out and grabbed Timon's tunic, pulling him to her. "I am Baroness Mikkotto from the House of Sumsumitoyo—a royal cousin of the House of de Magela. Surely you have heard of me?"

Timon felt deep fear. "I've heard of you."

"Yes, I can see in your eyes that you have."

"Baroness, we must not keep Aganess Jezra waiting," Hilkiah said nervously.

Ignoring the priest, Mikkotto pulled Timon even closer. "How fares Lady Maura?"

"You mean the pretender? I do not know, Baroness."

Mikkotto smiled. "Come, come now. Make it easy on yourself, Prince Bes. You can tell us what we want to know and dine sumptuously tonight, or you can suffer unspeakable pain and still tell us what we want to know. The choice is yours."

"I don't know what you want of me."

"We have the amulet. We know you work for Maura. We just want to know why."

"Why what?"

Mikkotto asked, "Why did she entrust the amulet to you and permit you to bring it into the temple of Bhuttu? Why would Maura run the risk of the amulet being discovered? Surely she must have realized the priests would sense the presence of the amulet. It doesn't make sense, my young man."

Hilkiah stepped forward. "We needed the amulet to set Zedek free, so why would she allow the amulet to leave her control?"

"You know where Zedek is?" gasped KiKu in a sarcastic tone.

"Silence! No one gave thee permission to speak," hissed Hilkiah. "Lashes across thy back will cure thee of thy insolence."

Mikkotto smiled. "I don't think I would waste my time on the Bilboa. My guess is no torture would be effective on him."

"Why not?" sneered Hilkiah.

"Because while you have been babbling, he has swallowed something. Probably poison."

Timon jerked free from Mikkotto and raced to KiKu. "Don't let it be true!" He peered into KiKu's strained face. "Don't leave me alone with these villains!"

KiKu's eyes rolled up into his head.

Grabbing KiKu's tunic, Timon began shaking him, "You coward! How could you?"

"I . . . was . . . commanded to . . ." gasped KiKu, slipping into unconsciousness and slowly sliding to the floor.

Timon caught the collapsing spylord and held him, weeping against the KiKu's neck. "Don't leave me! You can't abandon me!"

KiKu shook violently several times and went limp. His still-open eyes stared back at Timon as his mouth went slack and a thin trail of blood oozed from his mouth and down his chin.

Timon let out a piercing cry that filled the small chamber and echoed down the long hallway, holding KiKu tightly to his breast.

Mikkotto closed her eyes for a brief instant while she savored KiKu's death. She learned long ago that death was a useful tool in achieving her goals and vanquishing her enemies, even if it meant using her children as assassins—well, her male children.

Her daughters must survive at all costs. She had left them in hiding with a trusted relative in Hasan Daeg, where they awaited her triumphant return.

She straightened her pose while inserting her gloves into her belt and then beckoned to a sentry standing outside the cell. "When the boy stops weeping, bring him to the aganess. She wants to question him."

The guard returned the Bhuttanian salute and stood in the doorway.

Hilkiah squeezed past the large sentry to follow Mikkotto as she swaggered out of the cellar.

"What shall we do now?" asked the High Priest.

Mikado turned a lazy gaze upon the anxious, pale man. "If I were you, I would be making up a good story."

"What dost thou mean?"

"The boy's servant killed himself with poison. If he

truly was Zoar's traitorous hetmaan, the aganess will not be pleased to learn of his death. He would have been a fountain of information."

Hilkiah's face became livid with red streaks rushing up his neck onto his cheeks. His eyebrows arched high while his mouth took on an unpleasant shape. "Thou wast present as well. I wasn't the only one standing by while that creature swallowed poison."

Mikkotto smiled. "Not my temple. Not my responsibility." She pointed to the priest's chest. "I don't think the aganess will appreciate that you revealed the amulet." She whispered into his ear. "I believe it was to remain a secret. Now I'll have to kill the sentry in case he overheard."

"Oh, great Bhuttu!" exclaimed Hilkiah, grabbing Mikkotto's arm.

She scowled disdainfully at his chalky hand.

Hilkiah removed his hand quickly and pleaded, "Canst thou not help me? Of course, I would assist any endeavor thou seest fit in the near future, perhaps?" Hilkiah's voice had taken on a silky quality.

Mikkotto smiled. "I can think of something you can do for me right now. Let us return to your chambers and discuss it."

Hilkiah's smirk faded, since he knew of Mikkotto's reputation for deriving pleasure from engaging in practices that could prove painful to others, but he did not wish to anger the powerful woman. "It would be my honor, Baroness," Hilkiah assured, thinking he would just have to endure whatever Mikkotto had in store for him.

"After you," responded Mikkotto, bowing before the priest. As Hilkiah trudged to his chambers, Mikkotto signaled to her entourage waiting in the hallway.

They nodded.

When the two were out of sight, Mikkotto's Hasan Daegian women stormed the room, garroted the sentry, pulled Timon off KiKu's lifeless body, and spirited him away into the misty gloom.

Also by
ABIGAIL KEAM

Princess Maura Tales

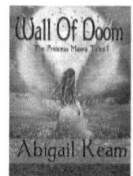    

Josiah Reynolds Mysteries

Last Chance For Love Series

DEATH BY MALICE
A JOSIAH REYNOLDS MYSTERY
Book 10

What do you do when your best friend
is out to kill you?

About The Author

Hello, my friend. I hope you are enjoying the Princess Maura Tales. I had such fun writing about Princess Maura and her adventures. If you like to read in other genres, I also write *The Josiah Reynolds Mystery Series* and *The Last Chance For Love Series*, a happily-ever-after sweet romance series. I would love to hear from you.
abigailkeam@windstream.net

If you like my stories, please leave a review and tell your friends about me.

Visit me at **www.abigailkeam.com**